I0570356

Dead Behind the Shed

Ashton Community Hospital, Volume 2

Nanci Race

Published by MFM Books, 2025.

Dead Behind the Shed

Ashton Community Hospital Series
Book

Nanci Race

MFM Books

Dead Behind the Shed
Copyright © 2025 Nanci Race
MFM Books
ISBN 979-8-9992304-4-7

Cover Design:	MFM Books
Pictures:	Depositphoto
Interior Design:	MFM Books
Editor:	Mary Marvella Barfield

Dedication:

This book is dedicated to Rich, Elizabeth, Donna, and Nicole, the nurses who sparked the idea for the series. Thank you to all of you and to my husband, Bob, who is my chief supporter. My apologies if I have forgotten anyone

Chapter One

Janessa eased out of the sliding doors of the emergency room entrance of the hospital before they were fully open. Determined to confront Margarite about smoking, she stomped toward the shed located at the backside of the hospital. All of the health system campuses were supposed to be smoke-free facilities, yet every day at break her best friend, Margarite, sneaked away for a cigarette. RN Janessa Williams, the self-appointed watchdog, resolutely kept walking until she was near the shed. She meant to stop her friend from ruining her life, at all costs.

If the senior management team caught her smoking again, Margarite faced suspension or worse, termination. Twice was bad enough. Three strikes and she'd be out. The nurses' union wouldn't be able to save her this time; and she, Janessa, wasn't going to let that happen.

"Margarite," Janessa called in a loud whisper. "Where are you? If Potts catches you again you are so screwed. Margarite! I know you're out here somewhere; I can smell the smoke." She reached the shed but didn't find her friend. Deciding Margarite must be around back and not answering, Janessa continued. "Margarite if you're back here you'd better answer me. Come on, answer. My break is almost over, and I've wasted it hunting you down. Where are you?"

The body rested against the back of the shed, which partially hid it. At first glance, Janessa thought it was a sleeping homeless person. As she got closer, she could see that the long auburn hair and slender build were that of a female. "Margarite!!" Janessa screamed and ran over to the body. She didn't want to touch her. She didn't want to move the hair out of the woman's face to verify that the dead body was her friend. "Oh Margarite, what have you done to yourself?"

"Spilled coffee all over my scrubs, that's what I did."

Janessa whirled around to see her friend standing about five feet away dabbing at her scrub top.

"What are you doing out here, Janessa? I only...holy moly! Is she dead?"

Janessa expelled her breath with a whoosh. *Thank God it's not Margarite.* She mentally chastised herself for thinking that way, but her friend was okay and that was the important thing. She turned back to the dead woman then reached into her pocket and donned a pair of gloves. After gently pushing the hair back, she checked the woman's carotid pulse in her neck. Nothing. No pulse, no chest rise. The woman was cold to the touch. It was a hot sunny morning in June, so she'd probably been dead for a while. Janessa scanned the body, but didn't immediately see any obvious wounds. When she had pushed the woman's hair back, she saw the red/purple marks on the neck, as well as the scarf knotted around it. It was no longer tight but hung loosely as if the killer wanted to make sure there were no signs of life and loosened it to check. She didn't want to look any further, so Janessa straightened and turned to Margarite.

"Margarite, call 911. This woman's been dead awhile. Judging from the marks on her neck she was strangled." Janessa looked around the area. "I'm not a coroner, but the ligature that was used is still in place."

"911, what are you talking about? We are 911. This is a hospital. You want me to call us? I can walk into the ER and tell someone."

"Not the time for jokes. Call the police, then page Carla. We need the supervisor out here when the police show up."

"Strangled? This is not good, Janessa. No one is going to believe that you're the one who found another dead body. This will be bad publicity for Ashton Community Hospital." She walked away shaking her head, dialing her cell phone. "Bad news. What will people say about us this time? Why does it always have to be you, why?"

Janessa ignored Margarite and pulled a small notepad out of her pocket. She glanced at her watch, noted the time, then deducted five minutes for the time she'd taken to check the woman's pulse and breathing. Her initial shock that it might be Margarite lying dead behind the shed was waning. Without missing a beat, Janessa craned her neck to see on the other side of the body, but refrained from walking around looking for clues. She was careful not to get too close and disturb the area. Although the police chief had warned her against investigating crimes on her own, she couldn't stop herself.

A few minutes later Janessa could hear the sirens nearing the emergency room. She glanced up to make sure the police cars weren't blocking the entrance. The ambulance still needed space to get in. Most of the people they brought in were still alive and needed emergency care to keep them that way.

Detective Lance Halen, Janessa's boyfriend, stepped out of his vehicle as Margarite came out of the emergency room door. Thundering behind her was the supervisor, Carla Potts. In her sixties, she was a big woman who towered over Margarite's five feet eight-inch frame. At about 160 pounds, Margarite was no match for the 200-plus, six-foot-tall Carla, nicknamed the "Amazon of Ashton." She had a loud, deep voice, faded red hair, and a pale face covered with freckles. She was built like a linebacker with broad shoulders and large hands that could probably palm a basketball. Although Janessa was used to Carla's abrupt, blunt manner, she still ground her teeth at the sound of the first screech. Carla had once been a top-notch NICU nurse before she decided to come to the small town of Ashton to take the supervisor job in the 25-bed Critical Access hospital. There had been some rumors of impropriety at her previous job.

"Janessa Williams!" Carla bellowed, "What in heck have you done this time? Margarite said something about a dead body." She stretched out her neck trying to see past the officer who was examining the corpse. "Oh my... Who is this woman? Do you know her, Williams?"

Janessa stiffened. She walked away from the police and the body to get closer to her boss. "No, Carla, I don't know her. For a few minutes, I thought it was Margarite lying there."

"Why would you think that? She's standing right behind me." Carla looked over at the woman again. "Oh, I see. The hair color is the same." Carla walked closer to the shed. "We need to find out who she is. Detective Halen, how did she die?"

Lance looked up. He was squatting next to the woman's body. Janessa saw him flinch when Carla's strident tone reached his ears. Margarite caught Janessa's attention and did an eye roll.

"I don't want to speculate. The coroner is on his way, but it might take him a little bit to get here. A call just came in that there's a traffic accident on Hightop Mountain and that's the way he'll be coming. So, he might be held up."

"What do we do now?" Carla persisted.

He stood, and although Carla was a tall woman, he towered over her. "We don't *do* anything. We can't move the body until the coroner gets here. So, the officers and I will stay with the body, and look for evidence. You ladies go back inside the hospital and go about your business. I'm sure you have sick patients that need your attention."

His gaze encompassed all three women, lingering on Janessa. When no one moved he waved them aside so another officer could put crime scene tape around the shed and the surrounding area. It appeared the discussion was over. He went back to his job, studying the body.

"But Lance, Detective Halen, I need to..."

"Carla, I'm only going to say this once. Turn *around* and *go* back the way you came. We'll let you know when we have any more information. Now take your nurses and get back into that hospital before I put you in my patrol car."

Carla looked as if she wanted to say more, but something in Lance's look must have warned her. Just before she turned away, Janessa caught his wink. She smiled and then caught up with Carla and Margarite.

"I'll never smoke behind that shed again. All I can picture is that dead woman with my hair and that's enough to stop me."

"Smoking?" Carla's face flushed bright red. "This is a *NON-Smoking* campus! You're lucky I didn't catch you or there would be a write-up in your file. Now get to work. Your break was over long ago." She stood with her hands on her hips, glaring at the two nurses.

Janessa and Margarite walked through the sliding Emergency Department doors, down the hall, and to the elevator. They were safely on the fourth-floor Critical Care unit before they dared to take a deep breath. They weren't afraid of Carla, the nurses usually ignored her, but neither could afford another note in their HR file. If they threatened Carla with the union, she'd back off. She had no intention of tangling with the Massachusetts nurse's union. However, Human Resources would push it to the limit. Reprimands in their files could spell disaster for their careers and they were just hitting their stride. Janessa had already been called to HR because of a dead body. This made two.

"I wouldn't let 'Bully Bill' know that you found that woman's body. You know what he said the last time you found a dead body."

Janessa whirled around to look at Margarite. "That was different. She was my patient, and too many people thought it was a natural death. Besides, are you psychic? I was just thinking about that. But you know Carla, she'll run to tell him then gloat. Anyway, what can he do? It's not like I killed anyone. I don't *plan* to find dead people."

"No, you're not psychic and neither am I. If I was then I would have known there was a dead body behind the shed, and I could have stopped you from finding her. Too bad they don't get killed elsewhere."

Janessa eyed her friend as they got off the elevator. "I doubt they had a choice. Besides, I went out there looking for you. I hope after this episode you'll stop smoking. You know it's not good for you."

"Episode? Finding a dead body isn't just an *episode*. And stop talking to me like I killed her. By the looks of her, she was dead long before I got to work this morning. As for smoking, well...let's just say I won't be smoking behind *that* shed anymore."

Janessa swatted her friend. "Margarite you are impossible. Now, enough of that. As soon as we're off work today we need to find out what happened to that poor woman, who killed her, and why. Right now, we have patients to take care of. Get to work. Or did you forget that we left Tiffany alone up here with four patients?"

"Wait! We need to do what? Here we go again. We're going to get into so much trouble. Again!" Margarite pulled Janessa back to her side when she began walking away.

"You heard me. As soon as our shift is over, we need to start sleuthing and find out what happened. We already know the police won't tell us anything so it's up to us."

Glancing up, Janessa noted that the unit secretary was listening and eyeing them suspiciously. When Margarite opened her mouth to speak, Janessa pinched her arm lightly and then shot a warning glance at the secretary. "We'll talk later. Word about the dead woman will get around this place very quickly. Keep your ears and eyes open and your mouth shut."

Later that afternoon, Janessa met Margarite at the time clock as they were punching out. "I have news. Margarite did you hear anything?"

"No, but I saw Carla the ogre and Bully Bill talking to the police. Neither one of them looked happy. I can't believe we're sleuthing again." Margarite continued questioning Janessa. "You've solved one murder. Do you think we can find out what happened to the woman behind the shed? What I mean is, *before* we get fired?"

Janessa grinned. "I don't know if we can solve this, but we're going to try. She deserves justice too. I heard that the woman's name was April Max and that she was wandering around downtown early yesterday morning. She apparently was in the pharmacy trying to get a fake prescription filled for Oxycodone. The pharmacist called the cops, but she disappeared before they got there. I'd say she took something and overdosed behind the shed, but I saw clear ligature marks on her neck and there was a scarf wrapped around there. From what I could see it didn't look like she put up much of a fight when someone attacked her. She might have been out of it. Her nails looked clean and although her clothes were torn, it looked like that was more from normal wear than a fight. So, she was taken by surprise when she was strangled."

"Good grief, but who led her up here? And why die behind the shed? I mean we have a perfectly good emergency room. People drop dead in ERs all the time. You think she was drugged first, then killed?"

"I saw ligature marks on her neck, but that doesn't mean she was conscious when she was dragged behind the shed and killed. She was murdered by someone, and we need to find out who and why."

"You saw all of that in five minutes? You're good. Maybe you should be the cop and not Lance, although I'm glad you two finally figured things out and got together. I saw the wink Detective Cover Model sent your way. He's getting very daring, isn't he?"

Janessa felt her face fill with heat but ignored Margarite's remarks about Lance. "I think she was out of it when she was strangled. You didn't see the marks from the scarf around her neck. I did." Janessa grabbed Margarite's arm to stop her from speaking. "You haven't heard the best part." She paused for effect, looking directly into Margarite's green eyes.

"What? Come on Janessa, you always take forever to get to the good stuff. Spill it."

"She was somehow connected to Bully Bill."

"What? How?"

"I don't know, but I sure plan to find out. Maybe he killed her. I overheard him talking to Lance about her. He admitted that he knew her quite well."

"Tell me again why we're investigating this? We're nurses, not cops. Janessa, you're good at sleuthing, you proved that after Lara Scutterby's death when you caught her murderer. But you're going to get us into so much trouble with this. The murder of a strange woman isn't any of our business. She's not your patient like Lara was. You aren't a suspect in her murder. You need to leave this alone, Janessa."

"Nope. No way are we leaving this alone. Especially if there's a chance she's connected to Carla or Bill. Those two are always against us for any little imagined error so if one of them is guilty then so be it. I intend to find out one way or another. Besides, what's gotten into you? You always want to sleuth with me. And the dead woman looked enough like you to be your sister. Or something."

"I know. Maybe it was seeing that dead woman with hair like mine that's giving me the creeps. That could have been me dead behind that shed. What if this was a case of mistaken identity and someone was after me and got her by mistake?"

"Don't be silly. Who would want to kill you? You don't have any enemies, do you? Is someone after you for an unknown crime?" Janessa smiled.

Margarite sighed. "Not as far as I know, but she did look like me lying there. Even you thought it was me. Right?"

"I did, but that doesn't mean someone was after you and got her. But I think that her looking like you is not a coincidence. I think she's connected to you somehow. We need to find out how."

Chapter Two

The next weekend, Margarite drove to see her parents. They lived in a small town in Connecticut nearly two hours from Ashton, Massachusetts. She left early in the morning, anticipating that the conversation she was about to have with them wouldn't be easy and would take a while.

Margarite parked her car in the driveway of her parents' two-story bungalow. Located a mile from the coast, where the family spent days picnicking and hiking, when the weather was good. Unfortunately, Margarite didn't get a lot of time to spend in the pleasant village of Bentor CT. She parked her Toyota Rav 4 in the driveway, got out and ran up the walkway to the front door of the house, and entered. Savory smells hit her nose, signaling that her mother was making a big dinner. She stopped for a moment to sniff the air and enjoy. The aroma of baked ham hit her. A growl from her stomach hinted at approval from that part of her anatomy. Margarite had called earlier to alert her parents of her impending visit and she guessed that her mother also invited her brother and his family over for a meal since he lived nearby.

She wanted to talk to her parents before he got there. She wasn't sure if her brother knew the circumstances surrounding her adoption. She needed time to have a private conversation with her parents. Margarite walked into the kitchen and inhaled. There would be mashed potatoes and green beans to accompany the ham as well as her mother's homemade chocolate cake for dessert. Her mouth began watering.

"Hi, Mom. Something smells good in here."

"Hi honey, I'm so glad you could get away for a visit. How was traffic on the Interstate? Bad? There's always so much on the weekends. It seems that everyone is in a rush to get home."

"It wasn't too bad. Are Charlie and Annette coming over with the kids for dinner? The twins? Daniella? Or is she at a sporting event this weekend?"

"No, her schedule is clear as far as I know. And yes, they are coming for dinner. But remember, dear, your brother wants to be called by his given name now, Trent."

"I'd forgotten. I've called him Charlie since I was little. Now he has decided to change his name. How odd. What time will they be here?"

Her mother checked the Fitbit on her arm. "Probably in 45 minutes to an hour. Why? Impatient to see them?" she smiled. "You know Trent is really his name. He only wanted to be called Charlie because he idolized your cousin."

Margarite laughed. "I'm always impatient to see them. I love spending time with the kids. Is Dad around? I need to ask you both something."

"I'm sure he's not too far away. He's already been complaining that he's hungry. He says his stomach is about to meet his backbone. I told him there's too much flesh and adipose tissue in between for that to happen and that he'd have to bear with it until everyone arrived. Was there something special you wanted to talk about?"

Her mother was very astute when it came to her children. "As I said, there is something I would like to ask you and Dad."

"What is that dear?" Her mother stopped what she was doing and turned to look at Margarite. A crease appeared between her brows. It always popped up when she was worried.

"Let me go find Dad. It's something I need to ask both of you."

At that moment, her father came around the corner, scooped her into his arms, and gave her one of his famous bear hugs. "Did I hear your mother say that I'm fat?"

"No dear. You just have a lot of excess tissue between your stomach and your backbone."

Margarite returned his embrace and kissed his cheek. "You look good, Dad."

"Not according to your mother. Too much around the middle. I keep telling her it makes me a better hugger. Having something to hold onto when you hug someone makes it so much better." He smiled at Margarite.

"I think you're perfect the way you are, Dad."

"What's on your mind, dear? Let's get whatever it is out of the way so we can relax and enjoy our time together." Her mother said.

"I know, Mom. This might sound strange, but I wanted to ask you about my adoption."

Margarite couldn't interpret the look that passed between her parents. They knew something and she was determined to find out what. Especially after finding the body of the woman who resembled her.

"What brought this on? Isn't this sudden?" Her mother asked. "You've never asked about it before." Her face flushed. "Not that we won't tell you what we know, I'm just a little surprised that you'd want to know now."

"There are several reasons I'm asking," Margarite said. "But someday I might want to get married and have a family. I might want to know my health history. And..."

"And what? Have you met someone? I know you mentioned a detective Cranston you started seeing. Is it serious?" Her father moved next to her mother, presenting a united front to their daughter. "You are our daughter. The person who birthed you gave up those rights when she signed the papers relinquishing you."

"Don't Paul, she has a right to know anything we can tell her about her birth family. Honey, we don't know much. We have a copy of your original birth certificate. It has your birth name, but most things in your birth records have been redacted. Yours was a closed adoption and apparently, they wanted it that way or all the information would be available."

"I understand that, Mom. But, with today's technology and DNA, it doesn't matter if the information on my adoption papers is redacted. I can still find out what I need to know. I thought it would save me some time if you had some information."

Margarite's mother sighed. "As I said, we'll give you what we have, but it's not much. What's the other reason you picked now to delve into this?"

Her mother's expression had softened, and Margarite knew she was adjusting to her request for information. "It's just that the other day, my friend Janessa found a deceased woman behind the shed at our hospital. I probably shouldn't be telling you this but..."

"What does that have to do with you, sweetie?" Margarite's father asked as he put his arm around her mother.

"Dad, Mom, the woman looked like me. She had my hair and was about my build. When Janessa saw her lying there, she initially thought it *was* me. We're trying to find out who this woman is. Don't you see? I need to know if I have any connection to her? Someone killed her and we don't know who or why. She might be a relative of mine."

Her mother gasped and then covered her mouth. She looked at Margarite who could see the horror in her eyes. At that moment, the front door opened, and Margarite's brother and his family arrived so she knew that for now, she wouldn't get any more answers. But that was enough for now. She could wait. Before the weekend was over, hopefully, she would be able to sit down with her parents and see if they could help figure this out.

"We'll talk later. Okay?" Margarite smiled at her parents.

She had to admit that the thought of the dead woman being related to her was frightening. Why was she killed? Did the killer mean to target her or was Margarite in danger as well? Who was April Max?

Who killed her and left her behind the shed at the hospital? And why did she look so much like Margarite? She hoped she could get answers to some of her questions this weekend. She hadn't told her parents the woman's name. Maybe when she did it would trigger a memory. She wondered if Janessa had gotten any answers to her questions. She'd promised to sleuth while Margarite was in Connecticut.

Margarite had a great time visiting her brother and his family and the cousins who drifted in and out over the two days she was in Connecticut. She decided that before she drove back to Massachusetts, she needed to talk with her parents again about her birth family. At this point any little tidbit of information they had might help solve, not only the mystery of her birth but also the murder of April Hill.

After breakfast on Sunday when all the other relatives were gone, Margarite and her parents sat at the kitchen table. "Mom, Dad? Can we talk about this situation that we have at Ashton Hospital? I have to leave soon. I don't want to drive back at night. It gets dark earlier these days. So, any information you have might help me figure this out. Besides doing a DNA test, I don't know what to do."

Margarite's mother slid a manilla envelope across the table to her. "I'm afraid this is all I have dear. It's not much, but a DNA test might get you what you need."

"Thanks, Mom. I didn't mean to spring this on you. It was such a shock when I saw that woman lying there. Her hair was the exact color of mine. From what I could see she was older but looked in good shape. At first, Janessa thought it might be drug-related, but now I'm not so sure. What if someone targeted her? I heard a rumor that she was at the pharmacy in town looking for drugs, but that doesn't mean it's true, but someone in Ashton knows something about her. That someone might also be her killer."

"Whatever it is, Honey, we're behind you in this search. We'll support you in whatever decisions you make. Remember that we love you and that you've been our daughter since you were an infant. Birth doesn't necessarily make someone family." Her father said, his face was wearing a serious expression.

"I know, Dad. I love you too. You've been the best parents I could have ever hoped for, and I will keep you in the loop. I promise not to shut you out of this whether the news is good or bad. Now, I'd better pack up my stuff and hit the road. Do you need help with anything before I go, Mom?" she asked as she stood up.

"No thanks, Dear. Your father and I can manage. He needs to get up, move, and do some work anyway," her mother said.

"Hey, I move around and work. What are you talking about?"

Her mother poked him in his slight paunch. "That, mister. We need to work on getting rid of that middle-age spread you've got going on there."

Margarite stopped and looked at her parents. "There is one other thing. The shift director at the hospital, Carla Potts. Have you ever heard of her or met her?"

Her mother and father looked at each other. They both shrugged. "I've never heard of anyone by that name. Why? Is she someone important?" her father asked.

Margarite sighed. "I'm not sure. She could be. I'm asking because she's about my build, but a little heavier, with faded red hair mixed with gray. Back in the day, she might have been closer to my coloring. Janessa pointed out a faint resemblance between us."

"This is getting complicated," Margarite's father said, getting up from the table and collecting the dirty dishes.

Margarite's mother also helped clear the table, before walking to the kitchen. "I have no idea who either of these women are, but Honey, we'll help in any way we can with your search for your birth family. In the meantime, please be careful. Tell Janessa to keep her eyes peeled too. We don't want anything to happen to either of you."

"Thanks, Mom and Dad. I'll call you when and if I find out more about the identities of the two women. I'm betting that Carla knows more than she's saying and that she's involved up to her neck with this murder."

A short time later, Margarite stood by the front door with her bags. "Who knows, maybe one of them is my birth mother, Margarite said as she hugged her parents. She left through the front door and walked over to her car. She waved to her parents who were still standing in the open doorway. After placing her bag in the car, she slid into the driver's seat. *I hope and pray it's not Carla Potts who is my birth mother. That would be the ultimate nightmare. Time to head back to Ashton, Massachusetts and the reality of murder.*

MONDAY MORNING IN ASHTON, Massachusetts was clear, but cold. Janessa finished dressing, ate a quick breakfast, and fed Brutus. She needed to drop him off at Nips and Yips Doggy Daycare on her way to the hospital. She hadn't spoken to Margarite over the weekend and she was anxious to hear what she'd learned from her parents. She hoped her friend had found out more information from them regarding her birth family.

The Critical Care Unit was quiet when Janessa walked through the door. Margarite arrived a little while later. The two-night nurses gave a quick, but thorough report at Huddle and soon Janessa and Margarite were busy with their three patients. Although they were stable, the nurses didn't have time to talk in between doing their routine nursing tasks. Patricia, the young nurse's assistant, was running back and forth, taking vital signs and doing the general work needed for the patient's comfort. It was hours before the women could take a break. The secretary wasn't due to arrive for another hour so the three of them had to cover the phones and anything else that came up that the secretary normally handled.

"Whew," Janessa said, mopping her forehead with a hanky. "What a morning." She tapped Margarite's arm, "Please tell me your weekend went well and that you got a ton of information about your birth family."

Margarite shook her head then sighed. "Not really. My mother gave me a manilla envelope full of papers to look over."

"What was in them?"

"I don't know. I didn't look at them. I couldn't bring myself to read them. I want you to be with me in case it's really bad."

Janessa reached across the desk and patted her friend's hand. "Of course I'll be there. I told you before, I'll be with you through to the end. You don't have to worry. You're not alone. In the meantime, we need to see if we can find out any more about Bully Bill's connection to our victim. I also think that Potts is in it up to her neck."

Margarite shrugged. "Why do you say that? I can't see the two of them working together on anything except to get rid of you on some trumped-up charge."

"I can't either, but I have a gut feeling. Potts has been acting very strange since I found April Hill. I have a feeling that there's some connection between the three of them."

"What does Lance have to say about it?"

Janessa stood. Her patient's call light was flashing. "I haven't had a chance to talk to him. He was swamped this weekend so he couldn't come over. Our phone conversations were cut short by Pete yelling for him to get a move on."

Margarite laughed. "Yup, that's my man all right. Always in a hurry. He wants everything done yesterday and is quite vocal about it."

Janessa eyed her friend. "I hope he's not in a hurry for *everything*." She laughed as the other woman's face turned scarlet, then she went to check her patient. She returned to find Margarite staring at the computer monitor as if it held the answer to all the problems in the universe.

"You know what, Janessa? Maybe Bully Bill and April were lovers. Maybe he killed her because she was going to tell his wife about their affair."

"Yuck. That's a pretty horrible thought and what does that say about our victim if she was having an affair with Bully Bill. And where does that leave Potts?"

Margarite looked pensive for a couple of seconds then looked at Janessa. A huge smile spread across her face. "A ménage á trois?"

Janessa clapped a hand over her mouth to stifle a laugh. "Stop, you're so bad. I can't unsee that visual. I think I might be sick."

"And what visual would that be Ms. Williams?" Carla Potts swept into the Critical Care Unit. "You'd better not be sleuthing. Margarite, Mr. Camprey's light is on and you're out here yucking it up with Janessa. Get to work and take care of your patients. That's what you're paid for."

The two women glanced at each other, shrugged and walked away from Carla who was still talking to them. Neither was ready to confront her yet.

Chapter Three

After Carla Potts left the Unit, Janessa and Margarite flopped in the chairs at the nurse's station. The eyed each other until a fit of laughter erupted from them.

"Wow," Janessa said, finally catching her breath. Margarite was still having difficulty controlling her laughter, so it was minutes later when she could talk.

"That was close," Margarite said. "We'd better talk about Potts when we're off duty. If she hears us talking and linking her with Bully Bill, we would be in trouble."

Janessa grinned. "Yes, but you have to admit that the thought of them together or in a ménage is hilarious. It's also a sight I never want to see. Seriously, we need to keep our ears and eyes open. Something is going on around here that's extremely odd."

"That is true. What gets me is how much that woman looked like me or rather, I looked like her. I have a gut feeling that there's a connection between us. I also hate to admit it, but Potts fits in there too. She might be a faded redhead, but she has my build and looks. It might be a coincidence, but I need to find out. God knows I don't want her in my family tree, but I might not have a choice. She knows more than she's saying about April Hill."

Janessa grabbed Margarite's hand. "You're sure your parents don't know Carla?" Margarite shook her head. "We need to look over the papers your parents gave you. There may be more information in there than we think."

"Yes," Margarite said. "But that brings us back to our original questions. Who killed April and why? Whatever is in the envelope my parents gave me, I doubt it will give us the answers to those questions. It might raise more."

Janessa smiled. "I'm sure we will have more after we see what we have in the envelope. On the other hand, there just might be a piece of the puzzle in there that will help us figure things out."

"I hope so. The more I find out the more questions I have."

"What questions do you have?" Janessa asked.

"Well, for one thing, I know my adoption was closed, but my parents don't seem to have *any* information. Unless there's something in that envelope to explain the circumstances of my birth, they seem to be as much in the dark as we are."

"It is hard to believe that they know nothing about your past. However, you were an infant when they adopted you. Maybe they didn't want to know any more than the fact that you were now their child. I doubt they wanted anyone from your past looking them up and trying to interfere in your life."

Margarite fidgeted with a paperclip on the desk. She bent it completely out of shape and then held it up to Janessa. "This is how I feel my life is right now. Completely bent out of shape and unrecognizable. Tell me again why looking into my ancestry was a good idea?"

"Well actually, we're looking into a murder that might be connected to your ancestry. One way or another we'll solve one of these mysteries."

"I hope we can solve this murder without one of us being interrogated as a suspect. Neither of us knew April Hill and I have to admit it gives me extreme pleasure to see Bully Bill in the hotseat. Whether he killed April or not. He knew her and the police know that."

Margarite shifted in her seat. "Where do we go from here? We know that Bully Bill is somehow involved with this woman. Whether he murdered her or not remains to be seen. I can't picture him as a killer."

"I agree. He may be a lot of things, but a killer isn't one of them. Although I will say that there are times that I know he wants to murder me."

"You're right about that.'" Margarite laughed. "I don't know who wants to get you more, him or Potts. You're not exactly on her best friends list."

Janessa stood and lifted her arms over her head to stretch. "And I thank God every day for that small favor. I can't imagine my life if the woman liked me and treated me as a fellow human instead of something lower than cow dung."

The women laughed, then sobered. "Seriously, Margarite, we need to look at the papers your parents gave you. There have to be clues about your background. Somehow you must be connected to April Hill. It might be a coincidence, but, I doubt it. I'm not a firm believer in coincidence and I don't think you are either."

Margarite nodded. Their conversation was interrupted when Patricia, the medical assistant came out of a patient's room and relayed to Janessa that the woman was a 7 out of 10 on the pain scale and would like something to help with that.

Janessa smiled at her, "Let me check her chart. I think Mrs. Drent is due for some pain medication." After administering the medication and making a note in the electronic record, Janessa returned to the nurse's station and her conversation with Margarite.

"I agree with you. Coincidence is not a reliable thing." Margarite said as Janessa sat down. "The pull was there for me from the moment I saw poor April lying on the ground dead. We need to move on this. Who knows the killer might come after me next."

"Do you have any enemies?" Janessa asked as she sat back in her chair.

"Not that I know of, but things happen. This has to be connected to my birth family. If April is a relative of mine, then someone wanted to shut her up about something. We need to find out who and what."

"What about your cousin? The PI. Have you spoken to him yet?"

"Cousin Charlie? I called him and left a message. He wasn't answering so I assume he's on a case somewhere. As soon as I reach him, I'll tell him about the situation and see what he can do."

"Great, in the meantime I'll reach out to our friendly neighborhood coroner and see when the autopsy results will be done."

Margarite stared at Janessa, her eyes widening. "Why? You and I both saw the ligature marks on her neck. It was obvious she was strangled. What could the coroner tell us that we don't already know? Although if he could tell us who did it and why, I'd kiss him for being a miracle worker."

Janessa shrugged. "I don't know at this point. Maybe I'm grasping at straws, but who knows what he will produce? He might find something useful. At the very least he can tell us about any drugs in her system and if the rumors are true that she was in the pharmacy in town days before her death, trying to get drugs."

"An identity would be nice. Yes, we know her name, but who is she? Why was she in Ashton? I've never seen her around here before. Have you?"

"No, Margarite, I don't remember ever seeing her before. But we both heard that she *was* seen in town at the pharmacy. Someone said she was trying to get drugs, but we can't prove that. That's why I'm anxious to get autopsy and tox screen results."

Margarite nodded. "Let's hope your friendly coroner doesn't suddenly develop a conscience and decide he can't tell us anything because we're not police. All I know is I've never seen her before. We need to make a plan."

"You're right. Let's make a list. 1. Send in your DNA sample for testing. 2. Read through your papers for clues. 3. Call your cousin Charlie, the PI again. 4. Call Frank Scott, to see if the coroner's office has gotten the autopsy report back from the medical examiner. 5. Keep sleuthing at the hospital. Is there anything I've forgotten?"

Margarite shrugged and wrinkled her brow. "I can't think of anything offhand. I think you covered everything."

"As soon as we are off duty we'll go to my house and call out for food, or we can make something simple for dinner. Then we'll take care of what's on this list. Oh yes, there's one more thing. 6. Catch a killer!"

"If only it were as easy as checking off an assignment on a to do list."

Janessa gave a mirthless laugh. "I don't think anything about this investigation will be easy."

Later that evening the women finished a meal of tacos, cleaned up, then sat at the kitchen table. Margarite placed the manilla envelope on the table, opened it and removed a sheaf of papers. Janessa noticed that Margarite's hands were shaking as she sorted the papers.

There was a sheen of tears in Margarite's eyes as she turned the top paper toward Janessa so she could read. One glance was all it took to show Janessa what she needed to know about the paper. It was a document from the court showing that an individual had relinquished custody of a ten-day old baby girl. The baby's name had been redacted as had the mother's name. There were so many redactions on the page that there were only a dozen words that were readable.

There were thick black lines through everything including the city or town of the birth as well as the hospital. It was evident that the birth parents took no chance of being identified in the future and the court sanctioned it by striking out all the relevant information. It would take a small miracle to find anything useful in the paper in front of them.

"My Mom said it listed my name, but I guess she forgot that it was redacted as well as every other important fact. Well, I guess that's it." Margarite said, dabbing at her eyes with a napkin. "There's no way I can find out who the people are that gave me up. They really wanted nothing to do with me."

Janessa placed a hand over Margarite's. "Hold on a minute. We don't know the circumstances. There are ways we can get around this paper. Have you sent in your DNA sample yet?"

Margarite shook her head, sniffed, and wiped her eyes again.

"Then get moving woman, and get that sample sent in. We're not going to know anything until you do. That at least will give us a clue about any familial matches. Then we can search until we find something. Right?"

Margarite gave a slight smile and nodded. "Okay, I won't give up hope yet. Let's see what other papers are in here." She picked up the next paper and smiled. "Here's my amended birth certificate and the change of name form where my parents named me Margarite."

Janessa took the paper from her hand and scanned it. "Look Margarite, it also says you weighed six pounds one ounce when you were born and that you were twenty-one inches long. No wonder you're so tall. You were a long baby."

Margarite laughed and pulled the paper out of Janessa's hand. "It also says my hair color was red too; in case you couldn't guess." The women laughed, then turned serious. "Although this is almost what I expected, it is a blow. But, as you said, we have other avenues to pursue. We also have a murder to solve."

"Absolutely. We need to find out about April. Who was she? Why was she at Ashton? And most important, who killed her? We're basically beginning from nothing and working in the dark on this one. Let me grab some paper so we can write down what we know so far." Janessa said.

Margarite dug a pen out of her purse and handed it to Janessa. "Okay we know or rather we've heard that April was seen in town at the local pharmacy earlier in the day, although we don't really know why she was there other than the rumors that hinted at drug seeking."

"Yes. We know that she was strangled." Janessa said. "That might have happened elsewhere. She might have been placed behind the shed later. Another thing we know is that she looks enough like you to be your older sister."

"Wait, do we know where the scarf that was used to strangle her came from? Was it hers? Or the killers? We also know that Potts has the same general features and coloring April and I have, but that's all."

"Also," Janessa said, "Bully Bill knew April and is involved somehow. He knows something. We need to find out what. And, you're right. We need to know where that scarf came from. It might have been hers. I think they might be able to gather some evidence from it."

Margarite laughed. "Do you really think that Bully Bill will tell us anything? He barely speaks to either of us except to berate us for something. He's especially out for blood when it comes to you, Janessa. Maybe you should have said yes when he asked you out."

"There's no way on earth I'd date a man like him. Now Dr. Lambert on the other hand is a different story. I might consider a date with him."

"Lambert? I thought you only had eyes for Detective Hunky. What would he say if he knew you were lusting after Dr. Lambert."

Janessa shrugged. "I don't think he'd like it very much, and I don't plan to tell him. I might look at Lambert and think wicked thoughts about him, but I'm all about Lance Halen. We've had several dates and we're getting pretty close. But, as someone once said to me, "Just because you're on a diet doesn't mean you can't look at the menu."

Margarite raised her brows. "Very funny. So, you and Lance are getting close? Have you?"

Janessa gasped. "Absolutely not! We're not at that stage yet and I think it will be quite a while before we get there. What about you and Cranston? Have you?"

"No way. We're taking it slow. I think he's my forever mate, and I don't want him skipping off somewhere because he thinks I'm easy. 'Cause I'm not."

Janessa got up and put on the kettle to make tea. "I don't believe for a minute he'd think of you that way. The man is gone, hook, line, and sinker. I wish we could bring the guys into our investigation. They have more resources than we do, but they'll just tell us to stay out of policework. While we have time, we need to plan our next move."

"Do we question Bully Bill or Potts? I would love the chance to ask her if she's a relative of mine or April's. Although I shudder to think she might be a relative of mine. If it turns out she is then I hope, it's distant. She's so awful. She's mean, pushy and lacks a sense of humor." Margarite said.

Janessa placed two cups on the table along with tea bags and honey. "She lacks most things that make up a human being. However, it won't help us find out who killed April if we don't talk to Potts as well as Bully Bill."

Chapter Four

The next day at the hospital, Margarite and Janessa were too busy to investigate anything. Patricia was working as their assistant again, which was good. There were four critical patients. When they did manage to take a break, Carla Potts and Bully Bill were nowhere in sight.

"If they thought you were sticking your nose in, they'd be on the unit in a flash. Start asking questions and stir things up a little. See what happens and get some action going." Margarite moved to her chair and sat down. "If we make them mad maybe one of them will slip and give us some information."

Janessa pulled out her chair and sat "How do you propose we stir things up and anger them without risking our jobs? Those two are on the hunt for my head so they can serve it to the board of directors on a platter."

"Do what?"

"Good grief, Margarite, have you been listening to yourself? How do we make them angry, so they slip up and give us information?"

"Oh. How do you propose we do that? You're the brains of this duo. You figure it out."

Janessa did an eyeroll. "I hardly think I'm the brains of the two of us. You don't want to talk to Potts, but if I have to question Bully Bill, you need to tackle her." Janessa grinned at her friend. She patted her dark curls. "After all, I'm not the one who looks like the gargoyle."

She laughed aloud when Margarite swatted her with a sheaf of papers lying on the counter at the nurse's station.

"Thanks for calling me a gargoyle. That's just wrong. What have I done to you to make you send me into the torture chamber? That woman is..."

"Coming into the unit as we speak. Jump up and look busy. I'm headed to Mr. Humphrey's room pronto." Janessa said as she left her chair and hurried into the patient's room.

The two women scattered. When the supervisor came into the Critical Care unit and walked over to the nurse's desk, Janessa and Margarite were busy attending to their patients. Their assistant, Patricia poked her head into the hall then ducked back into a patient's room following their lead. The nurses reappeared when they heard the receding footsteps of Carla Potts. Giggling, they came out of their patients' rooms and sat at the nurse's station to make notes. Patricia poked her head out of a patient's room and gave them a thumbs up before retreating back to her patient.

"That was close. We have to talk to her sometime but now is not the time. We need to make some plans first."

Margarite scratched her head. "Plans for what?"

"Good grief, Margarite. What is going on with you today? Snap out of it right now. Get your head in the game. Plans to question our two major suspects."

"Oh, yes. I see. So, what should we do? I've resigned myself to talking with Potts, but I don't have to like it."

Just then, Franklin Stevens, one of the housekeeping staff, walked into the Critical Care Unit. He gave them a wide smile. "Do you ladies mind if I clean up around here a little? Normally I wouldn't be here until the end of your shift, but I have to leave early today, and I didn't want to leave everything for the next shift."

Janessa smiled and nodded at him. "We don't mind at all, Franklin. Where do you need to start?"

"I'll start in the employee bathroom if that's all right. That room gets the most traffic, but is the easiest to clean."

"Be our guest. Just let us know if you need us to stand aside so you can get under the desk." Margarite motioned to the floor. "We'll gladly move for you."

Franklin nodded and walked away toward the bathroom. "Let's hope he doesn't come out with two vials of something. Speaking of vials, did you ever find out how they got into the Porter's closet in the Emergency Department when Lara Scutterby was killed?"

"Yes. I did." Janessa said. "I forgot to tell you that Emily confessed to the police that she thought about trying to kill Lara with Insulin. But she figured it would show up on a tox screen and that could point the finger at her. By then she'd already drawn up a couple of syringes full, so she wasted it in the sink and tossed the vials in the trash in the porter's closet."

Margarite sighed. "What a piece of work she turned out to be. And she planned to let you take the blame for all of it. Thank God, you caught her."

Janessa shifted in her chair. "I caught her all right. By the grace of God and a basin of vomit, I got her before she killed another patient of mine. I understand she's quite happy in the women's prison facility in Framingham, Massachusetts. She's welcome to it. Rather her than me."

Minutes later, Franklin returned to sweep under the desk at the nurse's station. The nurses shut down their computer screens and then moved to give him access after assuring themselves that no critical patient information was visible. Franklin cleaned counter spaces that were visible with a disinfectant wipe. He swept the floor under the desk and damp mopped a few spots. Franklin was done quickly. "Give the floor a minute or two to dry, then you girls can sit." He pushed his cleaning cart in front of him, waved and left the Unit.

"Thank God, no empty vials of anything," Margarite said.

The women resumed their shift, taking care of their patients and trying to make plans to sleuth in between. Janessa sat in her chair and looked at Margarite. "I'll find a way to talk to Bully Bill without raising his suspicions. That won't be easy, but neither will your talk with Potts."

"When do you plan to do that?"

"I'm not sure. Not today anyway. The shift is almost over. I want to pick up Brutus from Nips and Yips, go home, shower, and relax." Janessa said.

"No Lance tonight?" Margarite asked, a grin lifting the corners of her mouth.

"No, he and Pete are on a stakeout as if you didn't know."

Margarite laughed. By the time they ended their day, they were no closer to figuring out who killed April Hill and why. They planned to pull Margarite's cousin into the mix. He was a private investigator, with access to more information than the two women. He also had more time to dig into people's backgrounds. That's what he did for a living. Maybe he could figure out the identity of the killer.

Later that evening Janessa's phone rang. She and Margarite were making notes on the information they had. They also planned to go over the papers again in the envelope Margarite's parents had given her. "Hi, this is Janessa."

"Hi, Janessa, this is Charlie Piper, Margarite's cousin. She said you wanted to talk to me about a case you two fell into. You should get your PI license. Corpses drop like flies when you two are around. What do you have this time?"

Janessa filled him in, but he stopped her when she got to the part about the dead woman looking like Margarite. "Say that again, she looked like Margarite? My cousin?"

Putting the phone on speaker, Janessa sat down on her sofa next to Margarite. "She looked like her enough to be her sister or at the very least a relative. I'm telling you, Charlie, the red hair was the same and except for the death pallor and the ligature mark on her neck, you didn't hear that from me, you'd swear it was Margarite's twin. I think she was a little older than Margarite."

Janessa heard Charlie clear his throat. "You say you don't know how or why she was at the hospital? Did anyone else know who she was?"

"Yes. The head of HR, William Mager, knew her and we've figured out that the nursing supervisor, Carla Potts knew her as well. Margarite and I also noticed that although she's older and her red hair is faded, Potts resembles Margarite, which is strange. We've known her for several years but didn't notice the resemblance until after April Hill was killed."

"Well, you've given me a lot to think about. I'm working on a couple of cases right now. But your case intrigues me. Did Margarite talk to her parents?"

"Yes. They had little information. They gave Margarite an envelope of heavily redacted papers. Whatever you can dig up, along with Margarite's DNA, might be enough to figure out who this woman was. That also might tell us who killed her." Janessa answered.

"My cousin finally bit the bullet and sent in a DNA sample? She must want to find out if there's a connection between her and this dead woman if she is willing to do that. In the past, she refused. I'm glad she finally did it."

Janessa laughed. " Well, she's doing it now. Also, she can hear you, Charlie. I have the phone on speaker and she's sitting right here. I think she's more worried about being related to Carla Potts than she is the dead woman. Potts is horrible."

"Okay, kiddo. I'll see if I can find any information. It's too bad I don't know more about Margarite's birth." Charlie said. "Who knows, she could have a slew of relatives out there. Let's hope that more of them don't turn up dead. Or at the very least let's hope none are killers. Send me an email with everything you've found so far."

Janessa agreed, then she and Margarite said goodnight to Charlie. After she hung up the phone, she turned to Margarite. "I thought you were going to tell him about April. He seemed not to know. If he's going to look into this for us, we have to tell him everything."

"I was, but I knew you could articulate it better than me."

Janessa smiled. "Anyone who can come up with the word articulate can do it. You heard Charlie say this case intrigues him, so he'll start digging. He now also knows about the faint resemblance to Potts as well."

Margarite shrieked. "Potts, oh good grief, please don't let me be related to her."

"Better to find out now and get it over with. The resemblance is shallow. She might not have anything to do with you or your ancestry. Relax she's probably nothing to you."

"I sure hope not. I couldn't handle having her as part of my family. I wonder if she was born evil or if something happened to make her that way."

"You could be right, maybe something happened in her past that turned her into an uncaring, mean, and petty woman. I don't think she was born this way. These things take time to develop. I've read that overwhelming grief, or trauma can restrict a person's emotional response to events that you or I would find sad or uncomfortable. Whatever, they blunt their emotions from something they've been through. She might not be able to control how she feels." Janessa said.

"You almost make me feel sorry for her. I said *almost*. She should get counseling. *That* could humanize her."

Janessa laughed. "I'm glad that you're so understanding." She heard Margarite's derisive snort. "Honestly though, try being a little less judgmental."

Margarite's sigh was loud. "I'll try. I'm not making any promises though. If she gets too annoyed when I try to talk to her, all bets are off." She stood and pushed her chair under the table. " I'd better go now."

"Huh," Janessa said. "I think you got the better deal. I have to put up with Bully Bill. I don't want to have to beat him over the head with my father's name again. I thought I made my point with him, but he's thick-headed."

"Now who lacks compassion and understanding? He might have some trauma in his life that's made him behave this way toward you."

Janessa laughed. It was minutes before she got control of her emotions. "Yes, and I know exactly what his trauma was. I refused a date with the pompous, overbearing, *married* man. But you might be right. Maybe the death of April Hill is his trauma. *No*, he was like this before I discovered her body. When I spoke to him, he practically accused me of planting her body behind the shed so I could be the one to find her."

"I'm surprised he didn't accuse you of dying the woman's hair to look like mine."

"That's probably his next accusation when I see him. Which will be tomorrow. He doesn't work on weekends and tomorrow is Friday. Do you have any idea when you'll tackle Potts? You should do it soon."

"Tomorrow is as good a day as any. If you're talking to Bully, I'll track down Potts and see if I can ask her some strategic questions."

"Be careful," Janessa said. "She could be a killer."

"You need to be careful too. I don't trust Bully. He hates you enough to kill you, so who knows if he hated April enough to kill her." Margarite opened the front door but paused. "I'm scared Janessa. We need to find this person fast."

Janessa patted her friend's arm. "We will. It's been quiet around here since we found April. We haven't gotten any further in this investigation and it's been three months." She took a deep breath. "I'll see you tomorrow." She stood in the open doorway until Margarite was in her car and starting to back out of the driveway.

Chapter Five

The next day was sunny, but cool. Spring came and went, summer seemed even shorter in the Berkshires. Before long, winter would be headed to Ashton. April Hill's body had been found in late June. It was the beginning of September and Janessa still had no answers. She pulled her jacket tighter and wrapped her arms around herself as she walked to her mini-Cooper. Brutus trotted at her side. She looked down at the little dog. When he looked up at her, she swore he was grinning. "Yes, sweetie. Doggie daycare for you." He yipped with approval and leapt through the open car door. She harnessed him into the seat, and they were off.

She was dreading the day, which had barely started. Sometime today she had to talk to Bully Bill about April Hill. It wasn't a conversation she wanted to have. She knew that instead of answering her questions, he'd be furious and want to fire her for sleuthing. But that didn't matter. The important thing was to get information about the dead woman. What was her connection to him and what, if any, was her connection to Margarite? Janessa didn't envy her friend who had a similar task. She had to talk to their supervisor, Carla Potts.

Janessa arrived at the hospital. She was early so she couldn't clock in. The organization was strict about not clocking in too early or clocking out too late. Doing either meant seeing the supervisor about overtime and the staff wasn't allowed to leave early if they clocked in early, without special permission. Janessa used the extra time she had, to mentally go over what she wanted to ask Bully Bill.

As soon as it was time to clock in, Janessa checked into her unit and saw that the night nurses weren't quite ready for Huddle. She lifted the receiver on the desk phone and dialed the extension for Human Resources. She didn't expect Bully to be in this early, but she knew his secretary would be there. She wanted to schedule an appointment for later in the day.

"Human Resources, Nora speaking, how may I help you?"

"Hi Nora, it's Janessa Williams. How are you today?" The women exchanged pleasantries until Janessa decided to get to the point of her call. "I need to schedule an appointment with Mr. Magers. Does he have any openings after lunch? Say, about 1 or 1:30?"

"You're in luck. He has an opening from 1:15 to 1:25. Will that be enough time?"

Hmmm, 10 minutes. More than enough time considering I don't want to talk to him at all. "Yes, that's plenty of time."

"May I ask what this is about? Just so he knows and prepares himself if you have questions."

Janessa heard the secretary's faint laugh. *I'm glad she thinks this is so funny. I have questions, all right. He might not answer them, but I have to ask them anyway.* "It's a personal matter, Nora. I'd rather not get into it until I have a chance to talk to him. I'm sure you understand."

"Of course. I have you down for 1:15. I'll see you then. In case something comes up and he needs to cancel, you're working in the Critical Care Unit, correct?"

"That's right. You can reach me at extension 274. Thanks, Nora."

Janessa liked Nora. She was thorough and didn't pry into anyone's business. She also didn't consider Janessa to be a troublemaker like her boss did. If he felt that way before, God knew what he'd think after today's meeting with her. She expected fireworks. She hoped she had a job after she saw Bully Bill.

By the time she ended her call, Margarite was on the Unit and the other nurses were ready for Huddle. According to them they'd had one patient transferred to Reese Memorial Medical Center, Ashton's bigger, sister hospital. Janessa and Margarite had two more patients who were stable, the fourth patient had been moved to the medical unit.

"Okay, so the day begins. Who were you talking to when I came in?" Margarite asked.

"Nora in HR. I have an appointment with his highness at 1:15. According to her he can only give me 10 minutes and that's enough."

"Do you have any idea what you want to ask him?"

Janessa sighed. "I have a few vague ideas swirling around in my head. How about you? Have you contacted Potts yet to set up a time to talk to her?"

Margarite shook her head. "No, I..." At that moment, the light went on over a patient's room. "Saved by the bell."

Janessa heard her mutter under her breath as she walked away. Not waiting for Margarite to finish, Janessa went into another room and began patient care. Mr. Jax, the patient was in good spirits and informed her that he was being discharged today. Having heard this information at Huddle, Janessa smiled at the elderly man and finished cleaning him up and tidying the room. "When the doctor comes in then he'll give us a definite time that we can ship you out. Who will be picking you up?"

He grinned. "My wife Clarice. We've been married for 67 years. She's never let me down and if I know her, she'll be walking in that door very shortly." Sure enough, minutes later, his stooped, white-haired wife walked into the room. Janessa watched as they exchanged a kiss good morning. She could only hope for that kind of love. She and her boyfriend, Detective Lance Halen were still new in their relationship. In fact, he'd been so busy over the past couple of weeks they'd barely seen each other.

Lance, along with Margarite's boyfriend Detective Pete Cranston were busy investigating April Hill's death. They'd told the women to stay out of the investigation and leave the policework to them. However, if Janessa didn't think she and Margarite could help, she would stay out of it, but she knew that sometimes they could get into areas the police couldn't, thanks to Margarite's cousin Charlie. Janessa left the room, leaving Mr. Jax and his wife talking quietly. Mrs. Jax had pulled the visitor's chair close to the bed and the elderly couple held hands while they waited for the doctor to come and sign the discharge papers.

The nurses met in the corridor and headed for the nurse's station. As they sat down. They heard loud footsteps heading their way. "Good morning, ladies." Carla Potts' voice boomed through the small nurse's station. Out of the corner of her eye, Janessa saw Margarite cringe. *Good grief, how is she ever going to talk to her and ask her critical questions about April if she's scared of the woman?* Janessa wanted to reassure Margarite that everything would be okay. Hopefully, the killer wasn't the woman standing in front of them.

"Good morning, Carla," Janessa said.

"What's wrong with you, Margarite? You look like you've seen a ghost. I hope you're not carrying any disease. We certainly don't want to be contaminated. There's enough stuff going around this hospital without you bringing more in."

"G-good morning, Carla." Margarite stammered so much that Janessa looked at her. She was pale, a sheen of perspiration beaded her upper lip, which trembled. Good Lord, was her friend going to burst into tears?

"She has a slight headache, that's all. She took two Tylenol and should be fine in a few minutes. Right, Margarite?"

Margarite nodded and Carla seemed satisfied with their explanation. "Continue, I have other units to check on. I'll be back later."

Janessa heard rather than saw Margarite take a deep breath. "Are you okay? I thought you were going to pass out when Carla walked in."

Margarite dabbed her forehead and upper lip with a tissue. She offered a faint smile to Janessa. "I don't know if I can do it. You saw what happened to me and I barely spoke to her. What will I do when I start asking her questions? I know. It has to be done if we're going to get the information we need to crack this case and find out my true ancestry."

Janessa patted Margarite's arm. "It's okay. You'll get there. If we meet tonight and write down the questions to ask her, that will be a big help. You'll have something to go on instead of going in cold. Why don't you come over for dinner and after we eat, we'll go over the things we want to ask her. Now, it's time for lunch, I have to work up the nerve to talk to Bully Bill. Wish me luck with that one. I may be out of a job when I'm done." She smiled at Margarite to show that she was joking. Hmmm. *That might come true. I need to be careful.* She prudently hid her thoughts from Margarite who had enough to worry about. She could offer to talk to Potts herself but thought that Margarite should be the one to question the woman. Because she was quieter than Janessa, Potts might listen to her. It was a matter of figuring out what to ask so that Margarite didn't get on her bad side and shut them both down before they could start the investigation.

After a hurried lunch, Janessa took the elevator to Bully Bill's office. She was a little nervous, but Janessa wasn't afraid of him and what he thought he could do to her. She tapped on the door and walked in at his command. He sat behind his desk as if he thought he was a king or another figure of importance, but he looked like a giant puffed-up toad. Janessa had to erase that image from her mind, or she couldn't have a serious conversation.

"What do you want, Williams? I'm a busy man. I don't have all day to waste time on your chatter. So, get to it. "

He wants to be a jerk before I have a chance to speak. Well, he asked for it. Straight to the point then. "All right *Mr.* Magers. What was your relationship with Ms. Hill?"

Janessa watched his face turn purple as he sputtered trying to answer. "What business is it of yours? My personal life is not your concern. Now get out of my office."

She smiled and sat down in the chair opposite his massive oak desk. If he thought she would turn and run out the door, he had another think coming. "For reasons of my own, I'm making it my business. Please answer the questions. What was your relationship with the dead woman?"

"I thought I made myself clear. *That* is not your concern you interfering b... er ah busybody. Who I know and who I date is my own business. Now," he practically screamed, "Get out of my office before I throw you out."

Janessa had no doubt he thought he could physically throw her out. However, as big as he was, she didn't think he could do it. She and Margarite had taken a self-defense class while investigating the murder of Lara Scutterby, the daughter of Ashton Community Hospital's board president. There had been a special segment in the class on how to take down an opponent who was twice their size. Janessa estimated Bully Bill was four times her size, but she was sure she could inflict serious damage and pain on him.

"Calm down, Magers. I am aware that you knew April Hill. I didn't know you dated her. Thanks for that little bit of information. Were you married at the time?"

Janessa thought he was about to have a stroke when his face reddened even more. "How dare you insinuate that I would cheat on my wife with someone like April Hill?"

"Oh, come off it. When I started here you hit on me the first week. Remember our little elevator ride together? You've been ticked off ever since because I refused to date someone like you. You didn't mind cheating on your wife then. Did you suddenly develop a conscience, or did you have one too many close calls and your wife almost caught you?

I wonder what she'd say if she knew you tried to get it on with almost every new female employee."

"Shut up, just shut your filthy mouth. You know nothing about me or my life. You're just speculating and trying to trap me into admitting something."

Janessa tried to suppress a smile. She found the entire encounter with Bully Bill funny. She suppressed a laugh. She needed more information from him before he really kicked her out of his office. "Trap you? You can do that by yourself. I need truthful information from you. What did you mean by 'someone like' April Hill'? What do you know about her?"

Bill Magers was livid. Janessa waited for him to answer her question before he kicked her out of his office. It was a bold move on her part to accuse him of murder. She watched as his face turned a deeper shade of red then intensified to mottled purple. Again, she hoped he didn't have a stroke or a heart attack while she was there. She didn't want to perform CPR (cardiopulmonary resuscitation) on him. She always carried a CPR mask with her, but she was reluctant to use it on Bully Bill unless it was absolutely necessary. "I didn't admit to knowing the woman, you did, Bill. You said that you dated her. I merely asked if you were married at the time. Why are you afraid to answer my questions? Did you kill her?"

"Absolutely not! I haven't killed anyone. Did *you* kill her? Is that why you're accusing me? Trying to shift the blame away from yourself?" Janessa leaned back as flecks of spit flew out of Bully Bill's mouth. "I never said I dated her." He shouted. "Stop trying to put words in my mouth. She meant nothing to me."

"I'm afraid you did say that, and I believe you at least tried to date her. Does your wife know about her? What will she have to say if I ask her?"

Bill Magers stood up and leaned toward her, his hands on his desk. "Stay away from my family. I would never date a drug-addicted whore like April Hill. Now get out of my office!" He pointed to the door.

Janessa thought it would be prudent if she left at that moment. She wanted to ask him how he knew about April's drug use and why he called her a whore. Before she could think twice about it, she said the quiet part out loud. "Who said she was a whore? How do you know that? And," she paused to catch her breath, "How do you know she was on drugs? Did you supply them to her? Were you her dealer in return for certain favors she provided? It appears that you have an intimate knowledge of April Hill's life. I'll ask you again, did you kill her? If you didn't, do you know who did? Who wanted her dead other than you?"

"Get out of my office! You've gone too far. You won't get away with this one. I'll make sure you're fired and that you lose everything. I don't care about your daddy. He doesn't scare me. What I do is my business. Maybe I knew the woman, maybe not. That's none of your business."

Janessa edged toward the door. "Who was April Hill and where did you meet her? The police might be interested in your characterization of the dead woman."

Bill Magers pointed a finger at her. She noticed the tremor in his hand. "GO!" He bellowed.

She hadn't intended to get into a shouting match with him. All she wanted was information she could use to help her friend clear up the mystery of April Hill. It seemed as if all Janessa had done by provoking Bill Magers was to muddy the waters about April Hill's identity and purpose for being at the hospital. She was no closer to the killer than she had been when she started. She didn't think Bill Magers was the killer, but she thought he knew more than he was saying.

Chapter Six

Janessa walked to the elevator and hit the button to go downstairs to the Critical Care Unit. She wished she had better news for Margarite. She wished she had *any* news. Other than her suspicions that Bill Magers knew more than he was telling, he hadn't added anything to the investigation. The only thing she'd learned was that Bill and April had fallen out. He'd referred to her as a whore and a drug addict. It was an easy reach to say that she was a drug addict. Rumor had it that she'd been in town at the pharmacy trying to score drugs. Who other than someone with intimate knowledge of her would refer to her as a whore?

Perhaps the woman had rebuffed him, and he was calling her names because she was dead and couldn't defend herself. Janessa shuddered to think that any woman would let that slimy man touch her. Even if he paid her, would April Hill have let him? No one would ever know because someone thought it was a good idea to silence her forever.

The elevator dinged and she realized it had stopped on her floor. She walked over to the double doors of the Critical Care Unit, pulled them open, and walked through. Margarite was nowhere in sight, so Janessa sat in her chair and looked at the patient monitors. The Unit was quiet, so she had time to wait for Margarite to get back and get an update from her. She doubted anything had happened in the few minutes she'd been with Bully Bill. It seemed like it was forever, but when she checked her watch, she saw she'd been with him for about fifteen minutes.

Margarite walked out of the patient's room. "Hey," she said and smiled. "How did it go? Was it terrible? Did you want to turn and run out of the room? Was he as awful as usual or worse when you started questioning him about April?"

Janessa laughed. "Slow down. One question at a time. He wasn't any worse than usual, which is pretty bad. For a while, I thought he was going to have a stroke or a heart attack when I asked him if he'd killed her. His face was purple, with his eyes popping out of his head."

"He has those bulgy toad eyes anyway."

"This time it was way worse. Anyway, he denied that he killed her, which I expected. What I didn't expect was his characterization of her."

Margarite leaned forward to get closer to Janessa. "Which is what?"

"He called her a whore and a drug addict. I asked him how he knew that unless he had intimate knowledge of her. So, I asked him again if he killed her. He denied it again. But he knows something he's not telling. But I don't think he's our killer."

"Your what?" The shriek caught them unaware.

Neither of the women had heard Paula come through the door. They looked at each other. Janessa was sure the horror she felt was showing on her face and was mirrored on Margarite's. She shrugged. She figured they had nothing to lose at this point. "We don't think he killed April Hill, but he knows something about her death.

" Have you lost your mind? I hope you didn't actually accuse him, did you?"

Janessa was the first to regain her senses. "Yes, Carla, Bull...I mean Bill Magers knew April Hill. I just had a meeting with him and although he denies killing her, he knows something. He's not talking much, but he made his opinion of her obvious, which wasn't very good."

Margarite suddenly spoke. Janessa hid her surprise at Margarite's audacity with Carla Potts. She was usually the one throwing out jokes and clowning about almost everything. At that moment she was dead serious.

"What about you, Carla? We heard that you knew the victim too. We also noticed your resemblance, albeit your looks are somewhat faded. What's your connection to the *dead* woman?' Margarite emphasized the word *dead* when she looked directly into Carla Potts' face.

Carla's face lost all color. Janessa was afraid for a moment that Carla might pass out. Her mouth opened and closed like a fish sucking in food. Janessa almost laughed but gave herself a mental shake. Now was not the time to make fun of the supervisor.

Color slowly seeped back into Carla's face. She looked from one woman to the other before she spoke. "Let me set you straight, right now. Faded or not there is no resemblance between me and that...that woman. She was nothing to me." Carla's voice rose. "Nothing, do you hear me? Nothing." She turned to walk away, but although she was shocked by the supervisor's words, Janessa thought quickly.

"That's what you got out of what we just said? I can't believe you. A woman is dead and all you're worried about is if she looked like you? You knew her. How? You deny that she's anything to you, but she must be. Come on, Carla. We're not accusing you of killing her, although the way you're acting that would be a logical assumption. Why so defensive? I'm asking you again. What was your relationship with April Hill, who is now dead?"

Margarite and Janessa watched as Carla turned to glare at them. "Stay out of my business. It doesn't matter if I knew her. She's dead and nothing can be done about that so what does it matter now anyway? I'm not answering any more of your questions. You're not the police; you're just two nosy women, which eventually will get you into trouble or worse. I know you have work to do. Now get back to work, leave me alone, and stay out of this investigation."

Janessa couldn't resist. She wanted to ask Carla about the resemblance to Margarite. "But I need to know something, Carla..."

"No. Get to work. Williams, you'll be lucky if you don't get fired over this one. None of this is your business." Carla turned and left the Critical Care Unit.

The two nurses looked at each other. They both had grim expressions and at first, neither said a word. Finally, Margarite spoke. "Overall, I thought that went well, didn't you?"

Janessa couldn't stop the laughter that bubbled up and out. "Margarite, you are priceless. At the worst times, something pops out of your mouth that makes me laugh. You're right, that went well. If we think about it, we learned a lot from Potts." At Margarite's puzzled look, Janessa continued. "By Potts' reaction, we know there is a definite connection between her and April Hill. We might not know how or what it is, but we know it's something. Like Bully Bill, she knows more than she's saying."

"So, what's next? We need more than we have to connect the dots between Potts' resemblance to April and her murder. I don't think Potts is the killer. Or at least that's what I would like to believe. The only person she'd like to kill is you. Right?" She poked Janessa in the ribs and gave a small laugh. "We need more information, and I think we blew it with Potts and Bully Bill. They were the main leads in this investigation. Has Lance said anything?"

Janessa coughed and then grinned. "Lance? My close-mouthed detective boyfriend Lance Halen? Other than telling me to mind my own business, he won't tell me anything they've found. He says they're following up on a couple of leads, whatever that means."

"It means," Margarite began, "that he's not going to tell you any more than Pete is willing to tell me, which is nothing, and that we need to stay out of police business. When I reminded him that he told us that before and we solved Lara's murder, he reminded me that you were nearly killed because you didn't listen to him and Lance and let them do the investigating."

Janessa put her head in her hands and groaned. "Leave it to us to fall in love with a couple of cops. Why? Look where it's gotten us. Nowhere in learning who killed April Hill and why."

"I know. Okay, a break from this. We have a patient light going on. We need to get back to our jobs like Carla said. If she comes back and those lights are on, heads will roll. Ours."

"Lights?" Janessa looked down the hall and saw that another room's light was on. The women got up and headed for their patient's rooms. Fifteen minutes later the patients were settled, and the nurses sat down to document what they'd done in the electronic chart. It was good they were doing their work as Carla Potts looked around the corner of the door.

"Whew," Margarite said wiping a sheen of imaginary perspiration from her brow. "Carla is relentless today. She needs to stay in her lane. There's enough traffic over here. If she keeps it up, I'll tell her she has to take care of the patient's commode. If I tell her that's her chore for the day, we'll see how often she comes around then."

Janessa laughed at the mental picture of Potts cleaning out a commode. "She's just jumpy. After all, how often do you get accused of murder? She might not have done it, but I'll bet she has a good idea of who did." She looked Margarite up and down. "And...I think she's capable, so I'm not letting you out of my sight. We have no idea who's next."

Chapter Seven

The weekend came fast, and Janessa and Margarite planned a dinner at Janessa's with her boyfriend, Detective Lance Halen, and Margarite's boyfriend Detective Pete Cranston. Margarite was busy sampling crudités and cucumber dip. "What are we having for dinner tonight?" She asked. "Something smells luscious and I'm starving. I hope the guys get here soon."

"Hey, get out of the dip." Janessa lightly tapped her friend's hand. "We're having 'Drunken Chicken' with garlic mashed potatoes and green beans almondine." She heard Margarite laugh and she could guess why.

"Let me get this straight," Margarite said between gasps of laughter. We're serving 'Drunken Chicken' to two policemen? Aren't you afraid they'll arrest our dinner?" She broke into peals of laughter. She laughed so hard that she started coughing.

"Serves you right. I should let you choke," Janessa said as she handed Margarite a glass of water. "Drunken Chicken is chicken marinated in beer and a lot of garlic. By the time it's done all the alcohol is cooked off. It's flavorful meat, but it won't make anyone tipsy. The alcohol is gone by the time it comes out of the oven."

By now Margarite had herself under control. "I still wouldn't tell the guys what it's called." At Janessa's raised brows she laughed again. "Just saying."

"The men are off duty anyway. They won't be hauling our dinner away to jail. I'm sure they have better things to do with their time. Besides, I want to see if we can get any information out of them about their investigation into April Hill's death."

Margarite snickered. "Good luck with that. You don't believe they'll tell us anything, do you? Two tight-lipped by-the-book cops? No way. You can try, but I doubt we'll learn any more than we know already. And for God's sake don't say anything about the disastrous conversation we had with Carla Potts."

"Or the conversation I had with Bully Bill. My dad called me and told me to stop pushing Bill's buttons. He doesn't want to come and bail me out and get my job reinstated."

"You know your dad would be there in a heartbeat if he thought you needed him. And you and I both know Bully is terrified of making him mad. Ashton can't afford to lose their Chief of Surgery. They'll never find anyone as good as him and if he walks, no one will touch that hospital with a ten-foot scalpel."

Janessa wiped the counter with a damp cloth. "You're right. I don't want to get him in the middle of my war with Bully Bill, who's a slug that no one in their right mind likes. I wish I could find out what was his relationship with April." She tossed the cloth in the sink. "Let's go sit in the other room. Lance and Pete should be here any minute."

Before the women had a chance to sit, the doorbell rang. Janessa pulled a small portion of the curtain near the front door to one side to see Lance and Pete on the doorstep. She opened the door, grabbed their arms, and pulled them in. After shutting the door, she turned to look at them with a grin. "Hi, guys. You're right on time."

The two men looked at each other and shrugged. Lance was the first to speak. "So, you two are in trouble again, right? The way you pulled us through the door tells me something is up, and I bet it's nothing good. So, give. What have you done?"

Margarite walked over to stand beside Janessa. "What makes you think we did anything wrong?" She batted her eyes at Pete. "It's been quiet here. It's been quiet all week. Right, Janessa?"

"Yes. Quiet. Here and at work." She smiled at the men but couldn't quite meet their eyes. She shifted her gaze to a point behind them. "Would either of you like a drink before dinner?"

"Just water or iced tea if you have it. I'm driving," Lance said.

Janessa looked at Pete and waited for his response. "I'll have what he's having. You never know when you might get called out for something..., like for your girlfriend and her friend snooping into your murder investigation and ticking off the head of Human Resources."

"Yeah, or their supervisor, risking their jobs and potentially contaminating our suspect pool and wrecking our investigation."

Janessa swallowed hard and shifted her glance to Margarite. "How did you know? I mean we just had a couple of harmless conversations."

"Harmless conversations? Hmmm." Lance stroked his chin while giving both women a stern look. "So that's why Bill Mager called me to ask if you were collaborating with us on the investigation? Although I could barely make out what he was saying with all the yelling Carla Potts was doing."

Margarite's face was bright red, almost blending in with her hair. "Oh, that. There were small confrontations er... I mean conversations."

"Yeah," Pete said. "We gathered that from the shouting Bill and Carla were doing. Tell me this, Janessa. Did you accuse Bill Mager of murder?"

Janessa felt the heat rise on her face. "Not exactly." She crossed her fingers behind her back. "But he did seem to have details about April Hill's death. He knows more than he's telling. Something's going on and I think Potts knows something too."

Lance rolled his eyes. "What made you come to that conclusion?"

"It wasn't so much what they said, it's what they didn't say. They skirted the issue of how they knew April and what relationship they had with her. Potts even looks like her. Her coloring is faded, but you can still see a resemblance." Janessa said.

Lance took her arm and pulled her closer to him. With clenched teeth, he said, "Stay out of this. It's a murder investigation, a police matter. Don't you two get that? Stay..."

At that moment Janessa's phone rang. She'd left it on the coffee table. Lance picked it up before she could. He glanced at the screen before handing it over. "You'd better take this. It's your Private Investigator, Charlie Piper."

Blushing, Janessa took the phone from Lance and then glanced around the room. She didn't have time to wonder how Lance knew about Charlie. "Please excuse me, I need to take this." She walked into the kitchen and sat at the table. Charlie's timing couldn't have been worse, but there was nothing she could do about it, she needed to hear what he had to say. Maybe this was the breakthrough they needed to find April's killer. "Charlie, what's happening? Did you find out anything about April's death?" Janessa tried to keep her voice down so the others didn't hear. The last thing she needed was for Lance and Pete to know what she was up to although she was fairly sure they could guess.

"Hey, kid. I don't have a lot of information yet, but what I did find leads me to believe I'm on the right track. We don't have Margarite's DNA results yet, but I found a connection between the deceased woman and a cousin, Melanie Hill. She's fairly certain that one of her aunts had a baby and gave it up because the boyfriend dumped her. She has no idea where that baby was placed or which aunt it was. She comes from a large family with ten or twelve siblings and five of them were girls."

Janessa shifted in her seat to see if she could peek into the other room. "I may have to cut you off, Charlie. Lance and Pete are here for dinner, and you know what that means."

"Good grief, why didn't you say so? Anyway, Melanie is going to see if she can get any more information about her aunt and the baby she gave up."

"What about the father? Did she have any information about him? It would be so helpful if we knew who the father was. Then maybe we could figure out who killed April and why."

She heard Charlie sigh. "I'm afraid she couldn't help there, kid. All she could remember was that she thought his name was Steven or something like that. But remember she was quite young, so her memory is sketchy. As we get into this further, maybe she can find out more information. In the meantime, I'll keep digging. Go. Enjoy your dinner with the police." He laughed and hung up just as Lance chose that moment to walk into the kitchen.

"Something smells good," he said. Are we eating soon? Pete and Margarite are snuggling on the sofa and demolishing the dip and veggies."

"Yes, we are. Let me put out the food then we can eat." Janessa took the chicken out of the oven. She had placed it in there to keep it warm until they were ready to eat. I think you'll like the chicken, although Margarite is convinced you and Pete will either arrest us or the dinner when you find out what it's called."

She set the covered platter on the table. Lance came over to her and wrapped his arms around her waist. He nuzzled her neck causing her to lose her train of thought. "What? Oh, sorry, I forgot what you were asking."

He laughed, let her go, and turned her around to face him. "I asked what we were having for dinner, and you said we'd probably arrest you two. Is it that bad? Did you burn the dinner? Should I order pizza?"

Janessa laughed. "No. we're having 'Drunken Chicken,' garlic mashed potatoes and green beans almandine. Everything is ready so we can eat."

"I can understand why Margarite would be worried, but unless our dinner is driving down the road, she has nothing to worry about."

"Cooking the chicken makes sure that all the alcohol dissipates. It gets cooked off. The beer adds flavor without the intoxicating effects."

Lance pulled her into his arms and placed a light kiss on her lips. "That's just as well. You intoxicate me enough." He pulled her closer for a deeper kiss, but Pete walked in and cleared his throat. Margarite was right behind him. "I just thought we'd check on the food. We're starving, but I see why we haven't been served yet."

Janessa looked from him to Margarite's swollen, obviously kissed lips and laughed. "Guess you weren't starving a few minutes ago, were you?"

Margarite's face was bright red, and Pete's was only a shade lighter when they pulled up chairs and prepared to eat. Janessa placed the steaming bowls with the side dishes next to the platter of chicken and indicated they should serve themselves. A little later, everyone sat back in their chairs, sated from the delicious meal. Janessa put the kettle on for tea. She was thinking about having coffee, but decided it was too late.

Brutus lolled under the table after finishing his meal of doggie chicken and vegetables. Janessa figured he was hoping someone would drop a morsel for him, but no such luck. All the humans cleaned their plates. Margarite stood to help clear the table. Although the women tried to shoo the men into the other room, they refused to move and continued to sit in the kitchen while the women worked. The table was cleared, and the dishwasher was loaded in record time. When the chores were done, the men went into the living room. Janessa carried in a tray with cups of hot water, tea bags, and sugar, and cream if anyone wanted it. Behind her Margarite carried a tray with plates of pound cake topped with berries and whipped cream, a light and delicious dessert after the big meal they'd eaten.

As the evening progressed, the four friends talked about desultory things until it was time for the men and Margarite to leave. Janessa walked Lance to the door and after glancing around to see that Pete and Margarite were busy with their good nights, she gave Lance a warm kiss. He pulled her closer for another, but Pete chose that moment to say goodnight to the women. He said it loud enough to ensure Lance and Janessa heard him and separated. "This is the last time I will bring you with me," Lance said looking at Pete. He grinned, grabbed his arm, and pulled him out of the door. The women waved, shut the door, and collapsed on the sofa.

"I told Pete that I'm spending the night here. That's okay, isn't it?" Margarite asked as she picked up her cold cup of tea.

"Of course, you're welcome here anytime. It's too late for you to drive home alone and I knew you didn't want to ride home with the guys. Anyway, wait until I tell you what your cousin Charlie had to say. Come into the kitchen and we'll talk there."

Chapter Eight

"For pity's sake, Janessa, don't leave me hanging. What did Charlie say? Does he know who killed April? Does he know who my parents are and why they gave me up?"

Janessa laughed and put her hand on her friend's arm. "Whoa, slow down, girl. Charlie has a little bit of information. He doesn't know much, but it's more than we had before."

She watched Margarite fidget with her hands, interlacing her fingers, trying to hide the faint tremor as she sat at the table facing Janessa. They made more tea before they sat down. Margarite picked up her cup, then set it down without taking a sip. "Okay, tell me what Charlie said. And why didn't he talk to me?"

Janessa sighed, "This is exactly why. You can barely keep still. Pete and Lance would have known the whole story faster than you could get the words out of your mouth. Here's what Charlie knows. He found a woman named Melanie Hill. She had an aunt named April, but the family lost track of her years ago. The woman believes that this April, the murdered woman was one of her aunts. Melanie might be your cousin."

Margarite got up and dumped her cold tea in the sink and poured more hot water in her cup. She added another tea bag then sat back down at the table. "I see. What else did he learn? Does this Melanie know who I am?"

"I don't think so. Charlie says that when she was a little kid, she vaguely remembers hearing the adults talking about one of the aunts having a baby. The aunt gave the baby up for adoption. She doesn't remember which aunt it was, but she's said it might have been April who got pregnant and gave up a baby when she was very young. Melanie thought the aunt was an adolescent at the time she gave birth. It was all hushed up."

"Wow!" Margarite said. "Anything else? Does she know who my father is and if he's still alive?"

"Charlie said that all she could remember was that his name might have been Steven, but she wasn't sure. Her family didn't talk about him. There was trouble because of the baby. She never met him and has no idea what his full name is or where he might be."

Margarite sat back in her chair and sipped her tea. "If these people are my biological family, this is a lot to take in. Did Charlie know anything about the rest of the family? You said aunts so that must mean there's more than one. Where are they and who are they?"

Janessa got up to fix more tea. When she sat down again, she placed her hand over Margarite's. "From what he said, I gathered that Charlie didn't have much time to talk to Melanie. He's going to connect with her again. She promised to see what she could find out and let him know. He hasn't told her about you yet, but she questioned why he wanted information."

"What did he tell her?" Margarite asked.

"He told her about April's death and that he was a private investigator gathering information. He kept his answer vague. I know that as soon as April was identified the police contacted her family. The closest Charlie could come to family is Melanie. She hadn't heard from her family about the death, but from what Charlie says she's not in close communication with them. The police won't share any more information with him either. He says that he hinted to Melanie that the death might not have been an accident."

" I see." Margarite paused then asked, "And, why does it take so long for DNA results to come in?" Margarite asked. "I sent my sample in over a month ago."

Janessa chuckled "Says the woman who never wanted to take a DNA test in the first place."

Margarite got up from the table and put her empty teacup in the sink. "Yes, well, that was different. When I saw the woman lying there dead it changed my perspective about wanting to know who I am. I mean, she looked like me enough to frighten *you* into believing it was me when you first saw her lying there. I realized then that I wanted to know where I come from. My parents are okay that I want to search."

"I think in the long run you'll be happier knowing your origins." Janessa yawned. "I'm headed for bed. How about you?"

"Yes," Margarite said. "All this intrigue and drama is exhausting. I'm not sure I want to know what disasters will be waiting for us on Monday. We'll probably get attacked by Potts and Bully Bill."

"You had to plant that picture in my mind. I hope I can sleep without having nightmares about those two tonight."

Margarite walked toward the spare room after wishing Janessa a good night with no nightmares. She left the next day after the women had a breakfast of scrambled eggs, toast, and sausage. They had to work Monday, and, luckily, they were both in the Critical Care Unit on their regular shifts. By unspoken agreement, the subject of April Hill's murder would not be discussed while they were at work.

Monday was clear and cold. Margarite had errands after work, so the women decided not to carpool. Huddle was over quickly, and they did a check on their three patients and went about their routine jobs. As Janessa was preparing to leave Mr. Tidwell's room she heard a shuffling sound at the nurse's station. She walked out of the room and saw Franklin Stevens rifling through the papers on the desk.

"Is there something you need Franklin?"

He jumped and turned to look at Janessa. "No ma'am. I thought I would tidy up around here and help out. That's all. No harm done. I'm leaving."

Janessa watched him leave through the double doors. *That was odd. I wonder what he was looking for.*

Franklin was gone when Margarite strolled out of her patient's room. Janessa told her about the encounter. "It was a little creepy. I haven't a clue about what he wanted, he was..."

"Shhh," Margarite said. "He and Potts are right outside the door. It looks like they're arguing. They keep glancing this way and whispering." She nudged Janessa, "Quick, sit down, here she comes. Be prepared for questions." They sat in their chairs and logged onto their computers. The machines finished opening the patient information pages when Carla Potts walked into the Critical Care unit.

"Good morning, ladies. I trust everything is quiet today?" Carla Potts looked from Janessa to Margarite, her face devoid of emotion.

"Everything's fine Carla. Is there something we can help you with?" Janessa asked, not looking away from her computer.

"No. I'm checking in to make sure the patients are doing okay. We have three, correct?"

"Yes," Margarite answered. "Mrs. Humbolt, Mr. Plankett, and Mr.Tidwell. They're all fine. We just checked their vitals and as you see on the monitors everything looks good."

"Great. Then I'll leave you to it." Carla started to leave then suddenly turned back to look at the women. "By the way, pay no attention to Franklin Stevens. I know he can be a pest and a snoop, so I've assigned him to another area away from the patients and the patient information. He won't bother you again." After she made that announcement, she nearly ran out of the door.

There was stunned silence until Janessa shook her head and looked at Margarite. "What just happened?" Margarite shook her head. "Am I imagining it or were Franklin and Potts acting squirrely? What the heck is going on?" Janessa asked.

Margarite stood and looked down at Janessa. "I don't know, but I'm going to find out. That whole scene was bizarre. Do you think it has anything to do with April Hill?"

"I sure do. Those two are up to something and I don't like it. We never said a word about Franklin, but all of a sudden, he's assigned to another unit. Why?" Janessa shook her head. "And why was he lurking around here, poking around on the desk. What do you think he was looking for? What information could he need from this desk?"

Margarite shrugged. "You've got me. The man has only been here a couple of months and he's already in everyone's business. There's something strange about him. Face it, there's something strange about Potts and this whole mess with April Hill. I want some answers."

Janessa stood next to her friend. "I do too, Margarite, but we have to be careful. I'm not usually a conspiracy theorist, but those two are up to something, or they know something about this death. We'll get to the bottom of it one way or another." She patted Margarite's shoulder. "Hang in there. Nurses have to be critical thinkers. We have to think outside the box. We need to apply those principles to this problem."

"You're right. Guess we'd better get back to work and take care of our patients before Carla decides to come back and check on us again. Should we talk to Lance and Pete about this? Maybe they can help. They can ask questions that we can't."

"We have nothing to tell them. The police don't act on a hunch. They want facts and evidence, but we don't have any. Even this 'cousin' Melanie has no real information." She took a deep breath. "Besides, think about it. I have a sneaking suspicion they know what Charlie s we tell them we got information from your cousin Charlie, they'll blow a gasket."

Margarite sighed. "You're right. The less they know, the better. When we have something real then we can let them in on it. I have a sneaking suspicion that they know what Charlie is doing for us. You heard what Lance said when he handed you the phone the other night. 'It's your PI Charlie on the phone.'"

"I agree," Janessa said. "He did say that. They'll know soon enough. I have a feeling we're getting closer to the killer. We still don't know why April was killed, but I think once we figure out who is the killer, then we can figure out why he/she killed her."

"Tell me, Janessa, what do you think is going on with Potts and Franklin? That little scene just now was very odd."

"I know. He seems to be a quiet man, but there's something about him that sets off alarm bells. He bears watching."

Margarite chewed on her lip. "You don't think he could be the killer, do you? I mean he works here so he would have the opportunity."

"That's true, but I'm having trouble picturing him as a killer. Then again, you never know. Maybe he knew April and had a grudge against her."

"It's more likely that Potts had a grudge rather than poor old Franklin. She holds grudges against everyone, especially you. I suppose if she were going to kill anyone it would be you. Or at least she'd try with you. And then there's Bully Bill..."

Janessa snickered. "I wouldn't trust him as far as I could throw him. But I am leaning away from him being a killer. I don't think he has it in him."

Margarite sighed. "Well, it has to be someone. April didn't strangle herself. The most viable suspect we have right now is Franklin. We need to put our heads together and make a list of possibilities. There has to be another shady character in the mix. Who else was working the day April was killed?"

"Let me think. Darryl Mintz, the PA, was on duty. Dr. Kelleher, the hospitalist, housekeeping staff, including Franklin Stevens, Carla Potts, you, me, and Dr. Delsum breezed into the place. Forget the maternity staff, they were swamped. There were the nurses on the medical floor, but offhand I can't think of who they were. Let's get together and go over whatever list of names we can produce. Then I'm going to start questioning all of them one by one." Janessa said.

"And what about Bully Bill?"

Janessa laughed. "I already questioned him. I want to figure out who our killer is and why he/she targeted April. Is it just redheads or is there another reason? That's why I want you to stay close to me. You could be the next victim."

Chapter Nine

T hat night, Janessa and Margarite poured over the list they'd made of the people who were possible suspects in April Hills' murder. "We can eliminate most of the people on our list," Janessa tossed the papers aside. "Do you want something to drink, Margarite? I have soda, tea, coffee, or water."

Margarite sat back in her chair. "I'll have water. I don't understand why we can't focus on anyone. It's so frustrating." She glanced around Janessa's small kitchen. "Hey, where did you get that?" She pointed to a wooden plaque on the wall. It was about eight inches wide and roughly fifteen inches long; multi-dimensional flowers covered it. The colors were muted, but it was an eye-catching piece of art.

Janessa didn't have to look to see where Margarite was pointing. "My mom gave it to me. She painted it years ago. It's done with a long-forgotten embroidery paint called Artex. It was popular in the early 70s. My mom used it on many things like: tablecloths, napkins, and things like this painting. Like embroidery with thread and floss, she followed a design on fabric. When it dried, she cut it out, adhered it to the wood, and covered it with a clear acrylic sealer to protect the surface."

"It's beautiful," Margarite said as she took a bottle of water from Janessa's hand. "but we need to get back to what we were doing. Have you noticed that Franklin Stevens is hanging around more? What do you make of that?"

"I noticed. At first, I wondered if he had a crush on you, even though he's old enough to be your father. Now I'm not so sure. When I caught him rifling through the papers on the desk, I thought he was looking for patient information, until I spotted your purse, and he was eyeing that too. I think if I hadn't arrived at that moment he would have searched it. Speaking of that purse, you need to secure it when you come in to work. We have lockers for a reason."

"I know, but I was in a hurry, and it slipped my mind." She frowned. "Why would he be searching for information about me? Oh. I wonder if he has something to do with April's murder or if he knew her."

"I thought of that. I also noticed that you have his eyes. The shape and the color are identical."

Janessa watched as a horrified look crossed Margarite's face. "No way! Do you think he might be related to me? My father maybe?"

Before Janessa could answer, her phone rang. She looked at the screen before answering. It was the medical examiner. "Hi, Frank. What can I do for you?"

Frank coughed. "You did not hear this from me. April Hill was strangled."

Janessa interrupted. "I know that. I'm the one who found her, ligature marks and all. Tell me something I don't know. I'd like this case to be solved before someone else gets hurt. Namely Margarite. So, what else do you have?"

"The tox screen shows there were no drugs or alcohol in her system. I ran a few other tests and discovered that if she used drugs it had to have been a long time ago."

Janessa glanced at Margarite. "Rumor has it that she was in town trying to score drugs shortly before she was killed. How can that be?"

She heard the shuffling of papers. "Not true. She was clean. Where did that rumor come from? The person who started it could be either responsible for her murder or at least know the person who did it."

"I'm not sure who said it first, whether it was Carla Potts or Bill Mager. It might have been one of them, but I'm not sure which. I know it didn't come from the police."

Frank snorted. "They're the ones who asked me to do the other tests after I did the tox screen, but don't let on that you know. Maybe you can get your boyfriend to spill the beans about that. It's more than my job is worth for them to know that I've been keeping you in the loop. I heard that Margarite's resemblance to the dead woman is uncanny."

"That's true. We're hoping that Margarite's DNA results will be in sooner rather than later. Maybe then we'll get answers. If nothing else, we might be able to clear up the mystery of her parentage and if there is a relationship to April Hill."

"I'll keep digging. I know Margarite's adoptive parents and they're good people, but this is deep. I hope we find out the connection between her and the dead woman. I'll be in touch as soon as I have more information."

Janessa smiled into the phone although she knew he couldn't see her. "Thanks, Frank. I know you're trying. You're the best."

"Aw. I bet you say that to all the medical examiners you know."

She laughed. "Yes, I do. All one of you." Janessa turned off the phone and looked at Margarite. "That was Frank Scott."

"Janessa, you're the most exasperating friend I have. I know that was Frank. I'm sitting right here. I could hear you talking to him."

"I'm the only friend you have."

"Not true, but what did Frank have to say about April?" Margarite asked. She got up and put her bottle on the sink as Brutus wound himself around her legs. "I know sweet doggie. Your mommy is neglecting you. Don't worry, Auntie Mags is here. I'll take care of you." She picked up his water bowl and filled it with fresh water. She also took out the bag of kibble and filled his food bowl with his allotted serving. "Now, neglectful mom, what did Frank say about April?"

Janessa laughed and walked over to pat Brutus' head, but he was too busy with his food to notice. She glanced at her watch. It's time for his dinner, so, no neglect here. I was about to get his food and water when you intervened."

"Janessa!"

"Okay, he said that April didn't..." She turned to look at her front door when she heard a knock. Most people rang the doorbell. "Who on earth?"

She peeked around the curtain to see who was at the door then opened it. "Detectives Halen and Cranston. What can we do for you?"

Janessa watched as Lance and Pete looked at each other and then looked away. "Is it okay if we come in?" At her nod, the men strode into the living room and looked at the sofa where Margarite sat when she heard the detectives at the door. Pete Cranston walked over and sat next to her and smiled. Janessa saw her smile waver. Lance came in behind Pete and opted for the wing-backed chair. Janessa parked herself on the other side of Margarite.

"What's going on guys? You're still in suits and ties, are you still working?"

Lance cleared his throat before answering Janessa. "We've had a complaint against the two of you. We've been told that you've been harassing people and asking people about our victim."

Janessa was shocked, then angry. This woman's death might be connected to her best friend and that might put Margarite's life in danger. The police didn't seem to be getting the implications of how bad that could be. "Oh really?" She stared at Lance as if he'd grown horns. "And who has lodged this complaint? Or are you not at liberty to tell me?"

She turned to Pete whose face turned red before he looked away. Lance shifted in his seat and dropped his gaze before Janessa's penetrating stare. "Ashton Hospital's director of Human Resources called me. *Again.* I thought I asked you two to stay out of our investigation, but according to HR, you've continued questioning people about the death. Carla Potts even said..."

"Carla Potts! She's not part of Human Resources. Bully Bill is the one throwing his weight around in that department."

Janessa caught a hint of a smile that crossed Lance's face before he continued. "Carla was with him when he called the station to tell us what you've been up to."

Janessa snickered. "And I'm sure he embellished it to a fine degree, didn't he? I haven't spoken to either of them since the last time you told me to stay out of your investigation. Although I do have to see Potts, my supervisor, most days, I didn't mention April or her death."

Lance pulled a small notebook out of his pocket and flipped through a few pages before looking at her again. "According to my notes, you talked to the housekeeper Franklin Stevens. Were you questioning him about the death?"

"For crying out loud. No, we did not say anything to the housekeeper. We spoke to him about cleaning around the nurse's station..."

"And Janessa caught him searching through the papers on the desk. He was also eyeing my purse like it was a piece of candy. He's creepy," Margarite said.

"True. If I hadn't come out of the patient's room when I did, he would have been looking through her purse. I don't know why. However, Potts came in and dragged him out the door. It looked like they were having a huge argument."

Lance looked at Pete who shrugged. "Do you know why they were arguing? Did Franklin know April Hill? Is that what it was about?"

"How are we supposed to know that if we can't ask questions?"

Lance reached over and patted Janessa's knee. "Don't get riled. Pete and I are just doing our job. We need you two to stay out of this investigation. Someone could get hurt."

"Yeah," Margarite said. "I could get hurt or killed even. You guys don't seem to take that part of this too seriously. I could be next on the killer's hit list, whoever he or she might be. I'm not ready to die yet. I want us to find this person. I don't care who finds him or her."

When the men stood up to leave, the women followed suit. "Promise me you're not going to keep investigating," Lance said as he touched Janessa's arm. She looked up into his deep blue eyes and smiled. She grabbed his hand and wove her fingers through his. "I promise I won't keep questioning Potts and Bully Bill. And for the record, neither I nor Margarite ever asked any questions of Franklin Stevens. He started hanging around all of a sudden and he's been dogging Margarite. Potts took care of him. She said she assigned him to a different unit away from any patients. We'll see if he shows up again and starts sniffing around."

"Okay. I'm trying to keep you safe. After the last murder you solved when Lara Scutterby was killed, I almost had heart failure when I got to the hospital to see that Terry attacked you. If not for your patient's quick thinking by throwing the vomit in her face, you could have ended up with a lethal dose of Sodium Chloride coursing through your veins."

"You're preaching to the choir. I know how lucky I was when Terry attacked me. This is a different situation. This time someone might come after Margarite. I need to help protect her."

Lance pulled her close to him and hugged her. "You don't know that anyone is after Margarite. Let us do our job. Pete and I will keep both of you safe."

Janessa glanced over at her friend and her detective boyfriend Pete Cranston. They were in a lip lock that seemed to go on forever. Lance smiled and bent his head down to Janessa's level. "See? Pete is already on the job. No one is going to get past him to get to his girl. Same here." He lowered his head and gave her a searing kiss that curled her toes. When they came up for air, Janessa smiled at him.

"I thought you two were still on duty. I didn't realize that kissing was allowed."

He laughed. "All part of the investigation, honey. All part of the investigation."

After the detectives left, Janessa and Margarite started giggling like teenagers. Margarite thumped her friend on the back. "Nice deflection. I saw what you did."

"What?" Janessa grinned. "I'm not sure what you mean. All I did was say goodnight to the two detectives. One of whom happens to be my boyfriend."

Margarite deepened her voice. "Promise me you will stop investigating. Oh no, I won't ask Potts and Bully Bill any more questions." The women shrieked with laughter. "I bet it takes him until they get to the station before he realizes you never promised to stop investigating. You only agreed to stop questioning Potts and Bully Bill."

When the laughter died down the women went to the kitchen and sat at the table. Janessa stared in horror at the suspect list they'd left on the table. "Thank God the guys didn't come in here. Now, let me tell you what Frank said."

Chapter Ten

"Okay, talk to me. What did Frank have to say? Is there information that can help us with this non-investigation?" Margarite asked.

"Slow down, girl. Frank says April was strangled, which we knew. He also said, surprise, surprise, she had no drugs or alcohol in her system."

"What? You're kidding. Someone said they'd seen her in town earlier trying to score drugs. They said she was at the pharmacy asking about narcotics. How could she not have anything in her system? Is he sure?'

Janessa poured hot water into two mugs and added tea bags. She set one of the mugs in front of Margarite. "Not only is he sure, but the police also asked him to do some other tests because there was nothing in her tox screen. So, he tested things like her hair. Drugs or poisons will be retained in hair shaft and the roots. Frank says drugs can remain in the root for up to 90 days and can be detected within eight hours of use. April was clean."

"Wow. I don't remember where we heard the rumor about her trying to score drugs, but obviously that person was lying. Maybe they were trying to throw the police off the trail of the killer."

Janessa sipped her tea. "Well, that little ploy didn't work. Whoever it was didn't count on Frank. And our detectives aren't stupid. Those two guys have extensive training in a variety of areas. They were savvy enough to ask Frank to do the other tests for drug use. If I remember correctly, Bully Bill was one of the people who mentioned that April used drugs."

"That's right," Margarite said. She took a sip from her mug then put it on the table. "That was right before he kicked you out of his office and threatened your job."

Janessa laughed. "He threatens my job on a daily basis. I wish he'd wake up and smell the coffee. I'm not going anywhere. At least not before we figure out who killed April Hill, why she was killed, and if there is a connection to you, which I think there might be. I wish I could question him again. Maybe he'll slip and give me some information about her."

"There's no way you can talk to him. Remember what Lance said? You promised not to question Bully Bill and Potts. Let me ask you this, do we have any idea where Franklin Stevens came from? He's worked at Ashton for a few months, but I don't think we know much about him. Maybe we should find out a few things about his background."

Janessa stifled a groan. "I guess that means Potts and Bully are off limits. But," she giggled, "he didn't say I couldn't talk to Franklin Stevens or anyone else who might be a candidate for murder. Do you know where Potts has him working now? She said he was away from patients."

Margarite stared into space for a while. "The one place I can think of that she might have stashed him is on the floor with administration. No patients there and no access to any patient information."

"You're right," Janessa said. We'll check that when we get back to work. Right now, I think someone needs a potty break." She looked down. Brutus was under the table rubbing against her leg, one of the things he did to get her attention. When she stood Brutus wriggled from under the table and ran to the back door. He did his business once he was outside then danced around the door before whining to come back into the kitchen. Janessa refilled his water bowl, rubbed his head then sat down at the table. She stared at Margarite without speaking for a while.

"We need to think of a reason to be on that floor to talk to Franklin. If Potts catches us, we're toast. I bet he has all kinds of information about April. I can feel it," Janessa said.

"What you feel is Brutus licking your ankle." Margarite laughed.

Janessa got up, opened the cupboard, and took down a jar of dog treats she kept for Brutus. Dog friendly peanut butter treats were his favorite. She gave him one then sat back down to resume her conversation with Margarite. If you can think of anything, please let me know. My mind is drawing a blank. As I said, if Potts catches us, it won't be good, but we have to talk to him. He knows something, to say nothing of the fact that you and Franklin have the exact same eye color and a few of your mannerisms are similar."

"I'd rather be related to him than Potts. She's an evil woman. I don't think I've ever seen her smile. Have you?"

"No. I can't say that I ever have. She's just straight up mean all the time."

Margarite laughed. "Especially when it comes to you. She really doesn't like anything about you. She and Bully Bill would love to find a reason to get you fired."

"I know. But our immediate problem is finding out who killed April. The list of potential killers is shrinking thanks to the police and the people I can't question."

Margarite's sighs sounded loud in the quiet house. "I'm sure the guys think what they're doing is for the best. I don't think they believe that my life could be at risk."

"I agree. After talking to Potts and Bully Bill, things aren't what they seemed. I would love to know why he thought April was a drug addict. If he were intimate with her, he would know that, but maybe he was just trying to smear her name. I doubt Bully Bill uses drugs so there is a mystery."

Margarite stood, walked over to the sink, and put her cup inside. At that moment Janessa's phone rang. She held up a hand to signal for Margarite not to leave. "Hi Charlie. Do you have any good leads?"

"Boy have I ever. Is Margarite there?"

"She is, Charlie, I'm going to put the phone on speaker." She hit the speaker button. "Okay, what do you have for us?"

"Remember the cousin, Melanie?"

"Yes. Does she have more information?"

"She called me. She remembered that the aunt who had the baby was named...Are you ready for this?"

"Come on Charlie, you're killing us with the suspense."

"Okay, okay. Her name is Carla."

"Oh my God," Margarite shrieked. "Potts is my mother!"

"Okay, Charlie, now that you've got Margarite in a tizzy, is the one named Carla the mother of the baby or not?"

"Janessa, I'm not sure and neither was the cousin. She remembers the name Carla but thought she was either the one who had the baby or she was heavily involved at the time."

"Involved? What do you mean involved?" Janessa asked. She was looking at Margarite whose face turned three shades of red while Charlie was talking.

"She thought that Carla was the one who fixed everything. She made all the arrangements and everything. Her other thought was that the baby was Carla's, and she gave it away."

Margarite moaned and put her head on the table. "You need to find out more facts before Margarite goes insane." Janessa said eyeing Margarite. "You know we work with Carla and it's not pretty. 'Witch' would be one of the milder names we've called her."

"Tell Margarite not to get her panties in a twist. I'll find out one way or another. Melanie will dig a little deeper and get the facts."

"Right. I told you I have the phone on speaker. She can hear you."

"Oh, that's right, you did," Charlie said. "Sorry, Margarite. I'll do my best to dig up more information. We are making headway even if you aren't happy with the results. I'll talk to you ladies when I get something else."

Janessa said goodbye and clicked off the phone just as Margarite lifted her head. Janessa noted the glimmer of tears on her face. She sniffed, got up from the table, and grabbed a tissue from the box on the counter.

"Well, that was a terrible phone call. I could have done without that. I shudder when I think that horrible woman might be related to me. I'm praying she isn't. I couldn't stand it if she is related never mind the possibility that she might be my mother. You can't tell anyone about this, Janessa. Promise me."

Janessa looked at Margarite like she'd sprouted another head. "Who on this earth do you think I'd tell? Although I think you should alert your parents to the possibility."

"No. Absolutely not. Until I find out she's a connection, I don't want to upset them any more than I have to."

"But now is when you need their support. You need to lean on them while this gets sorted out." Janessa said. She walked over to the refrigerator and pulled out two bottles of water. "Here, this will help you think more clearly."

"Water does that?"

Janessa laughed. "I have no idea, but it took your mind off your problems for a minute and it's cold so that alone might help."

"You know," Margarite said after taking a sip of water. "I think it's helping. Who would have thought water is a magic elixir that could take away your troubles."

Janessa smiled but looked at her like she'd lost her mind. "Water is good for the most part, but I don't think I'd call it a magic elixir. Except if you're dehydrated. Then it's a cure-all."

"My point exactly." Margarite stood and got ready to leave. On that note, it's time for me to go home. I'll see you at work tomorrow unless Potts has done something screwy with the schedule. She's good at that."

"I know. I need consistency. I don't need to jump all over the place at that hospital. I have too much on my mind to deal with her shenanigans right now. She should leave well enough alone and not put her evil spin on things."

The next day, Janessa walked into a chaotic scene. Margarite was standing, hands fisted at her side, face red and fury glinting in her eyes. Across from her, looking equally as fierce, was Carla Potts. Trouble was brewing, and Margarite was angry. It couldn't be good.

"Why is it, Carla, that every time things are on an even keel, you have to come along and ruin everything? You and I know there's no reason to put me on 7 PM to 7 AM. This department is doing fine with Janessa and me running things here. What is your reason for assigning me that shift? Why, when it's not necessary?"

If possible, Carla stood straighter, making her body look more like an Amazon. Margarite was tall and good-sized, but Potts had a way of diminishing people. "Are you refusing to do your job, Ms. Barrett?"

"You'd like that, wouldn't you? I'm not refusing anything. I want to know why you suddenly decided to put me on nights. I deserve an answer."

Carla took a step closer to Margarite. Their faces were inches apart, neither budging an inch. "I said you're working nights, so you'll work nights. You do not question my authority. Unless you want to lose your job, you'll do as I say. Understand?"

"No, I don't understand. You throw your considerable weight around and expect us all to jump. I'll do my job, but don't think this is the end of it."

"There's nothing you can do about it, Barrett. What I say goes. Don't expect your buddy Williams to help you out with this one. Her job is on the line too,"

Janessa thought this was a good time to intervene. "My job is on the line? Since when. You'd better look at your job, Potts. No one is indispensable. Keep that in mind."

Carla Potts turned to look at Janessa who noticed Margarite smirking behind Carla's back. "Are you threatening me, Williams? When I go to HR with this bit of insubordination, you'll be fired. I've been waiting for this moment."

"Yeah, yeah. You do that Potts and then you can go to Leo Scutterby and explain why his Chief of Surgery has resigned. I hope you're prepared for the fallout from that. You can also tell him you had the woman who solved his daughter's murder fired."

Carla shook her fist at Janessa. "You won't get away with this you little b...witch. She whirled around to face Margarite. "And you'll work nights for as long as I want or you're out the door.

Chapter Eleven

J anessa walked over to Margarite and put an arm around her shoulders. "*She's* the witch! I can't believe she has the nerve to start threatening us. We can't let her get away with it."

Margarite pulled a tissue from her pocket and dabbed at her eyes. "I don't think there's much we can do about it. She *is* our supervisor. We have to do what she says or risk losing our jobs."

"Let me worry about Potts. Just do your shift. I'll do what I can to get you off nights. It's not safe for you to work that shift without me. That's what Potts wants, for you to be afraid and alone. I will check in with you as often as possible to ensure nothing is happening."

Margarite sniffed and wiped her eyes again. "I don't like it, Janessa. I'm scared. Suppose the killer comes after me. I have no protection against anyone."

Janessa pulled Margarite around to face her. "That's not true. Remember the self-defense class we took? Just think about all the moves we were taught. That's what saved me from Terry when she tried to kill me. A move we learned in class helped me disarm her."

"You were good in that class. I remember some of the things we were taught. I should have practiced a little more with Pete."

Janessa smiled. "Keep that in mind for the next time you two are together. I'm sure he'll be happy to give you some pointers."

"That's if I live through the next few nights. No one else is scheduled to work with me. Potts says if I get busy, she'll send over one of the maternity nurses. They have more nurses than patients. If they're having a slow night, why couldn't one of them work nights instead of me?"

Janessa sighed. "Unfortunately, this is the unit we work on most of the time. We know it better than anyone else. If one of us is available, then there's no way Potts is going to call in any other nurse from another department. It will be fine. I'll check in with you regularly. If you do have trouble, you can call security too. Griff Lewis is working nights. He might be the director of security and maintenance, but he does his fair share of the work, especially if one of his men is out sick. I'll give him a heads up that you're working solo."

Margarite sat down heavily in the chair at the nurse's station. "I'm glad Griff will be around. He's a good guy. I can breathe a little easier knowing that he can run up to the unit at a moment's notice if I need him.

"I'm glad he's on too. We'd better get to work before Potts comes back. When do you start the night shift?"

Margarite looked ready to cry again. "Day after tomorrow. Mr. Jenks and Mr. Tassone are scheduled for discharge today. If there are no further admissions, then I should only have Mrs. Phenot when I come back, but she might be discharged as well. However, you never know who will get sick and be admitted, so I'm going to psych myself up in case I have a couple of patients. Maybe I won't have time to dwell on what could happen."

Janessa was quiet. Margarite looked at her, waiting. When Janessa saw Margarite frown, she said, "I wonder why Potts didn't schedule anyone else to work 7 PM to 7 AM. That's a bit unusual. Anything could happen in this unit."

"She claims that she'll be around to help out if there's a problem or I can call over to maternity for backup, but I don't trust her for a minute."

"Me either," Janessa said. "But there's not a lot we can do about it right now. I'll get to work on the problem and see if I can fix this. Let's get to work. We have patients to care for."

The nurses went into the patient rooms to begin their respective treatments. They prepared the two men for discharge and settled Mrs.

Phenot, who was doing well. She had been placed on blood thinners after having a blood clot enter her lungs. She would remain on the medication for a time. The doctors were running tests to try and pinpoint the cause of the clot, especially since the patient was under 40. They suspected it had been caused by another drug she'd been taking, but until they finished the tests the doctors couldn't be sure. They decided to keep her in the Critical Care Unit for a while longer.

Janessa and Margarite met at the nurse's station when they were finished. "Why don't you take a break, Margarite? I can manage things here until you get back. I don't think either of the doctors will be here this morning. They'll probably pop in this afternoon to write the discharge orders. I made sure both men ordered lunch."

"Sounds like a good idea. You'll be okay on your own?"

Janessa smiled. "Of course. Collect your thoughts. Have tea or coffee and a snack. It's quiet at the moment."

Mrs. Phenot's call light over her door flashed. She was usually a quiet patient, so Janessa sauntered into the room. She increased her pace when she found the patient twisting the sheets in the bed. Her face was ghostly white, and she was grasping her chest. "Oh God, the pain is awful. Make it stop, nurse, please. It's so hard to breathe."

Janessa immediately checked the woman's vital signs. Her pulse was weak and thready. She noted the sheen of perspiration on the woman's face. Using the new paging system, Janessa pushed the button to summon the doctor and then called Margarite back to the floor. Dr. Lenno ran into the room. He was followed by Carla Potts. After checking the patient and ordering blood tests and more medication, Dr. Lenno left the room. When he came back, he said. "I've called for a portable X-Ray. Mrs. Phenot, try to relax. I think the clot has moved, but we'll get everything under control."

Carla Potts motioned for Janessa to come into the hallway. "You'd better hope I don't find out you neglected this patient and caused this. The last thing we need is for another patient to die on your watch."

Janessa stared at Carla Potts. "What are you talking about? I'm not the one going around killing people. The patient is in the Critical Care unit for a reason. She has a medical issue, which I have *not* caused. *You* are the supervisor. Stop berating me. Do your job and supervise."

Carla did an about-face and stomped into Mrs. Phenot's room. Janessa watched as she tried to project an image of calm, however, her face remained beet red, her fists clenched at her side. The door to the Critical Care Unit opened. Margarite rushed up to Janessa.

"What happened? I leave the floor for two minutes and all of a sudden there's an uproar."

"Mrs. Phenot had a bad spell. I'm not sure what happened. Dr. Lenno ordered bloodwork and a portable chest x-ray. He suggested that the clot had moved. She's taking blood thinners so I'm not sure what he'll want to do next. By the way, watch out. Potts just stomped into the room. She's on the warpath and practically accused me of trying to murder Mrs. Phenot."

Margarite shook her head. "Good grief. She's insane. Why would you kill a patient? I'll go in and see what's going on. Maybe you should check on the men and make sure they're okay."

Janessa smiled. Margarite was the calm one holding everything together. "Good idea. I'll be back in a couple of minutes." The two men seemed unaware of the drama happening down the hall. After checking on the men to be sure they were all right, Janessa went to the hall outside Mrs. Phenot's room. Margarite came out minutes later. "The x-ray shows that the clot has shifted in her lung. Luckily it hasn't gravitated to her heart or brain, but Dr. Lenno says it could if we're not careful."

"What is he planning to do?"

Potts came out of the room, looked at the two nurses, took a deep breath, and briefly closed her eyes. "Dr. Lenno has decided to let the blood thinners and anticoagulants do their job. For now, he wants to wait and watch. He hopes the clot will dissolve and not migrate to other parts of her body."

"I'll check with Dr. Lenno to see if there's anything special, he wants us to do." Janessa said as she returned to the patient's room. She'd only taken a few steps when she heard Carla Potts' give a derisive snort.

"I hope you keep a better eye on her than you've been doing. We don't need any further incidents. You have a way of putting patients in jeopardy."

Janessa couldn't let Carla's remarks go without a rebuttal. She knew she should keep quiet, but she didn't pause to think. She turned, walked back out, and shoved her face so close to Carla's that they were nearly touching. "Lara's death was hardly my fault," she said through gritted teeth. "I had no way of knowing that her *half-sister* wanted her dead. I'd never met Lara until the night she was killed. And I just met Mrs. Phenot. Now find someone else to harass and let me do my job."

"I'm warning you, Williams. Don't mess with me."

Janessa stared at the older nurse. "Or what? You'll report me to your buddy in HR? Go for it and see how far either of you gets with that. You and Mager are *not* at the top of the food chain."

Carla walked out of the door without another word.

"I thought so," Janessa said to the woman's retreating figure.

Margarite sighed and touched Janessa's arm. "What do you think she'll do? She's pretty angry with you right now. The look on her face. Evil, pure evil."

"At this point, I don't care what she does. We have patients to take care of and we can't let her stand in our way. She's worse than Bully Bill because she's sneaky. He's mean in an obvious way. We need to watch our backs with her. That's why I'm worried that you're working nights with her. I have a feeling she'll do something to get to you."

"I'm not afraid of Potts. I can hold my own against her." Margarite shrugged. "Besides, what can she do to me?"

"Probably more than we know. She is our supervisor and she's forcing you to work nights. Alone. She'll find a way to get at you because of me. I feel it."

Janessa turned and walked into Mrs. Phenot's room while Margarite walked over to the nurse's station and began writing notes. The two men were being discharged later. When Janessa returned, she flopped into the chair beside Margarite. "Dr. Lenno wants to keep the same orders he had for Mrs. Phenot. The only addition for now is he wants more frequent chest x-rays to monitor the clot."

"Isn't he afraid it will travel quicker than we can treat it?"

"He says he doesn't think it will. He thinks the medications are doing their job, and he wants to give it more time. He doesn't want to do any invasive procedures unless he has to. So, we'll wait and see what happens. I'm cautiously optimistic that he's right. Mrs Phenot's a nice woman. I wouldn't want anything to happen to her."

Margarite nodded. "Me either so I hope he knows what he's doing. I'm glad you were here with me. I shudder to think what nights will be like with just me and the 'wicked witch.'"

Janessa smiled and patted Margarite's arm. "You'll be fine. Remember the self-defense skills you were taught if you run into trouble. Mrs. Phenot will not be discharged today, so you'll have her to take your mind off things. I also spoke to Griff Lewis. He knows you'll be alone. I didn't get into detail, but the security rounds will be stepped up so they can come here more often to check that you're okay. He said that he'll be taking that shift because he's short-staffed. He's a good man, very conscientious," she said, but her smile was forced.

"I hope so, Janessa. I can't say I'm not worried because I am. The way this place has been lately, who knows what will happen."

"You'll be fine. We have systems in place to protect you." That was easy to say, but did she believe it?

Janessa and Margarite strolled out of the hospital at the end of their shift after Huddle. The two men they'd had for patients were discharged, leaving only Mrs. Phenot, who was stable and doing well. "Now don't forget, Margarite, if you have any problems call me immediately. I don't live that far away. I can be here in minutes."

"I thought you said I'd be fine. Now my anxiety level is back up again."

Janessa laughed and swatted Margarites arm. "You will be fine. The downside is that you'll have Potts wandering around. Good luck with that. I'd be more afraid of her than anyone else."

"But you said you didn't think she was a threat. Is she a threat or not? I know I have to watch my back with her because the least thing that goes wrong and she'll be talking to Bully Bill. He'd love that. If he can't get to you then the next best thing is to get to me." She looked over at Janessa, her beautiful green eyes shining with tears that were ready to fall.

"She won't do that. It's me she wants to fire, not you. You're one of her best nurses." She put her arm around Margarite as they walked to Janessa's Mini Cooper. "Just remember that I am nearby, and Griff Lewis has promised to step up his rounds and keep an eye on you. I trust him to do the right thing."

"Okay. I'll be strong. It's only for a few nights and if Griff is prowling around then it will be okay. I have to believe that."

"It will, I promise. When this is over, we'll look back and laugh over our foolishness. When was the last time you talked to Pete?"

Margarite smiled. "Last night. He's working nights with Lance. We have a dinner date scheduled for a couple of weeks from now. We should both be back on days by that time. At least I hope so. You don't think Potts will keep me on nights for long, do you?"

Janessa frowned. "No, I think she'll make you do a couple, maybe three nights to punish us. She wants to punish you for mouthing off to her about working nights and me for daring to stand up to her and question her authority. Once she gets over that then you'll be back on days. You'll see. This won't last long." Janessa hoped that was the case. If

Margarite were on nights longer than three days, she didn't know what they'd do. It was going to be hard to keep an eye on her and keep her safe for even one night let alone three or more. "Okay, let's get out of here. I've had enough of this place for one day. I still have to come back tomorrow. You get to sleep in." Her smile was a half-hearted gesture that she forced herself to make. She didn't want Margarite to see how worried she was.

Over the next two days, Janessa texted Margarite often to make sure she was okay. On the third night, Margarite sent a frantic text about Franklin Stevens. He was on the unit and Margarite was frightened. Janessa called the Critical Care Unit directly.

"CCU, Margarite speaking."

"I'm so glad you answered. Tell me what happened with Franklin Stevens."

"Janessa," She heard Margarite breathe deeply as if she was trying to catch her breath. "Franklin was here, pretending to clean. I asked him what he was doing. He claims that his supervisor told him to clean up here. When I told him that he was supposed to be on the bottom floor he acted angry and said he'd go where he wanted, and no one could tell him otherwise. He went about his business as if I hadn't said a word."

"What did you do then?"

"I called Griff. Thank God for the new alert system we have. He was here in minutes. He told Franklin to get back to the ground floor where he'd meet him. He said that Franklin isn't even supposed to be working nights."

"Good grief. Keep a close eye out for him. I haven't trusted him since the day he started at Ashton. There's something shady about him. He could be the person we've been looking for. You did the right thing. Call Griff if you have any other problems. Stay safe, Margarite. Make sure you let Potts know what happened."

"I did. She went right downstairs, She's out for blood. Glad I'm not in his shoes. I'll keep you posted. Don't worry. I think I'll be okay now. I'll talk to you later."

"Goodnight, Margarite. I'll talk to you sometime tomorrow."

Soon after Margarite hung up the phone, she heard a strange thump and thought she heard the door to the stairs close. She ran into Mrs. Phenot's room to make sure the woman hadn't fallen out of bed. She was going home tomorrow. They didn't want any accidents that would delay her departure. The woman was a sweetheart who wanted to get home to her family. Mrs. Phenot was safe in bed. Margarite heard the thump again and decided it was coming from the cardiac rehab room. She couldn't imagine that anyone would be in there at this time of night.

She tiptoed down the corridor and walked into the room. All the lights were off including the small light that was always left on at night. Margarite felt along the wall for the light switch and was abruptly shoved from behind. Before she had a chance to cry out, something struck the back of her head. She was vaguely aware that something was being wrapped around her neck and was shutting off her air. She clawed at the cloth trying to loosen it to get air, but blackness enveloped her. Then there was nothing.

Margarite's first thought when she woke up on the floor was, *I'm not dead, am I?* Noise rushed at her from all sides. She sucked in as much air as her lungs would take. Hands gently lifted her onto a gurney. Her vision was still hazy. She could make out figures of people but couldn't distinguish who they were until she heard Janessa say, "You're okay, Margarite. I'm here. Just relax and let the doctor take care of you."

Chapter Twelve

Margarite was admitted to the Critical Care Unit for observation. She had and IV in one arm and an oxygen mask in place. Detectives Halen and Cranston as well as a couple of other officers were at the hospital when Janessa had arrived. She wanted to start questioning people, but with the police there she couldn't. Like it or not she was going to investigate as soon as they finished and left the hospital. Someone tried to kill her best friend, and she needed to find out who that person was before they hurt someone else. As she stood waiting outside the room where Margarite was being examined, she heard a noise behind her.

"What are you doing sneaking up behind me? And where were you when someone was trying to kill Margarite? You're the supervisor, so you're responsible for her well-being. If Griff hadn't been making his rounds specifically to keep an eye on Margarite, she'd be dead now."

"*You* had better moderate your tone, Williams. I'm the one in charge, not you."

"Yes, Carla and you've done a fine job of it too. A nurse is almost strangled on your watch, and you casually saunter onto the unit without a care in the world. Do you have any idea who did this?" When Carla didn't answer, Janessa continued. "Of course you don't. And you call yourself a supervisor."

"You've said enough, Williams. I was busy in another unit when I got called to come here. Some of us try to do our jobs instead of standing around causing trouble and criticizing others."

"I'm not on duty tonight, you are." Janessa knew she was too angry to say anything more to Carla. Instead, she walked over to where the two policemen were questioning Griff Lewis.

""When I came into the unit, I didn't see nurse Barrett, so I thought she was in with a patient. I didn't realize all the patients had been discharged. I was just about to leave the unit when I heard noises coming from the Cardiac Rehab room." He paused and looked around. He gave a tight smile when he spotted Janessa, before continuing with his story.

Detective Lance Halen was taking notes in a small book. "Did you get a look at nurse Barrett's attacker? Anything that stood out to you? Was it a male or female?"

Griff shook his head. "I couldn't tell. The person was big, but they could have been either sex."

Janessa glanced back at Carla then looked her over from head to toe. As she continued to stare, the supervisor shook her head and stomped into the room where Margarite was still being examined by the doctor. Janessa turned back to the conversation between Griff and the detective. "I couldn't see the face or anything that would tell me who the person was. They wore a dark gray hoodie with a cap underneath the hood. It was pulled down to partially cover the face. The attacker also wore gloves and big boots."

"Boots?" Detective Pete Cranston joined the conversation.

"Yes." Griff continued, "you know those big, black, steel-toed work boots. That struck me as odd. The boots were almost outsized."

"Do you think the attacker was wearing bigger boots to throw us off his trail?" Janessa asked, moving closer to the detectives. She spotted Carla Potts sliding out of the room Margarite was in. However, the woman was too big to slide anywhere. "That is maybe the person wore boots a size bigger than their foot so we wouldn't be able to tell if they were male or female." She looked down at Carla's footwear then back up at the other woman's face, which was bright red. Unfortunately, the supervisor was wearing a pair of professional clogs. *She could have changed. She had time. And Carla is as big as a man.*

"At this point, Ms. Williams, we have nothing but speculation. We still have some more questions for Ms. Barrett before we file our report."

"I'd like to be with her while you ask your questions, if I may."

Lance smiled. "I don't see any reason you can't. I heard someone say that she's been asking for you. I think she'll be more relaxed if you're there. Maybe she'll remember something that can help us catch the guy."

Janessa couldn't stop herself. She turned a stared into Carla Potts face. "Or woman. Remember, this could have been a woman."

"Ms. Potts, we need to talk to you too. Please stay in this area until we finish talking to Ms. Barrett." Janessa turned to look at Carla's face while Lance was talking to her. Other than a red complexion, her expression was bland. She nodded and walked over to the nurse's desk.

Janessa walked into the room to be with Margarite. She stepped close to the bed, grabbed Margarite's hand, and gave it a light squeeze. Pete Cranston had come into the room and was on the other side of the bed lightly stroking the top of Margarite's other hand, being careful not to dislodge the IV.

"Thought I was dead. Next time maybe not so lucky." Margarite whispered.

Janessa tried to shake off her fears as she looked down at her friend. "Don't try to talk, honey. I'm going to stay with you for as long as I can."

"Work." The word came out as a raspy croak, but Janessa understood what Margarite was saying. "Yes, I have to work in the morning, but I want to stay at least until I know who's going to be working the floor and until you're settled. Just rest for now."

Dr. Lenno stood off to the side of the room and began to have a whispered conversation with Lance. Their conversation filtered over to Janessa.

"Obvious signs of bruising, but she was lucky. The attacker could have done severe damage. We have no patients in the Critical Care Unit, so we'll keep her here for observation. I assume that the supervisor will be able to find another nurse to take care of this unit."

Janessa masked her emotions. I don't want Margarite to be more frightened. As long as it's not Carla, Margarite will be safe. I thought I could eliminate her as a threat, but I don't trust her. Something is off about her.

Janessa patted Margarite's hand. "I'll be right back. I need to talk to someone."

"Not Carla," Her voice was hoarse. She strained to speak.

"No. Not Carla." Janessa said. "I'll deal with her later. She never should have left you alone. I told her it was risky, yet she did it anyway." When Janessa entered the hallway, she saw Barbara Cleason, one of the Maternity nurses talking to Carla. She looked around and spotted Griff as he was getting on the elevator. "Griff, wait up. I need to ask you something. Good thing the doors were open, or I wouldn't have seen you leaving."

"What can I help you with Ms. Williams? I hope Ms. Barrett is going to be okay. I got held up in another department or would have been here sooner. Maybe I would have caught the guy."

"You did your best, Griff, and we appreciate it. Margarite will be fine thanks to you for saving her. She called me before her attack. She said that Franklin Stevens was here, in the unit. He claimed that you told him to clean up here, although Carla told him to stay on the lower floors and away from the patient units."

"I never told him to come up here. I was fine with him working on the lower floors. He came up here on his own and lied to Ms. Barrett. I don't know what he was after, but he's been warned to stay away from the Critical Care Unit. Hey, do you think maybe he was the one who attacked Ms. Barrett? Maybe the police should ask him where he was during the attack."

"They will, Griff. Thank you for everything. I wanted to check to see if Franklin was supposed to be here. You confirmed that he wasn't. I'll give that information to the detectives."

Griff nodded then turned toward the elevator. Before he could push the button, the elevator doors opened revealing Franklin Stevens flanked by two uniformed officers. Janessa followed as they went into the empty room Lance and Pete were using to question people. No one spoke while they waited for the detectives. The two officers refused to let Janessa come into the room. She peeked around the door frame to see if she could spot Franklin. She thought if she looked at his face, and he was guilty, she could tell, which she couldn't do if she wasn't allowed into the room.

Janessa sighed with relief when Lance and Pete exited Margarite's room. She pointed to her right. "Franklin Stevens is in that room with the two officers. They wouldn't let me in."

"You can't be in there Janessa. We need to question him. You can't be in the room. You're not a policeman. You're also biased against him."

Janessa fumed. "But...but you let me be in the room with Margarite and Griff. Besides, Margarite called me before her attack. She said Franklin was in the Unit. He was told to work on the lower floors and stay away from here. Also, just so you know, he works days, not nights. And another thing, why would you think I'm biased?"

"Are you finished? Yes, we let you stay with Margarite for moral support. Your friend had just been attacked, nearly killed. She needed you more than she needed to be questioned. Pete and I didn't think she would tell us much in her condition. That's why we let you in the room with her. And we know about Franklin."

"How?" But Lance turned away from her and began walking to the other room. "Fine. I'll go back to Margarite." She turned her back on the detectives and marched into the room with her friend." She knew she was being childish when she heard Lance chuckle as she walked away. She softened her features as she neared the bed. Margarite's face was nearly as white as the sheets she was lying on. Her eyes were closed. Janessa battled tears as she looked down at her best friend. Margarite's eyelids fluttered. She looked up. She attempted a smile. "How are you feeling Mags?" The old nickname, unused for a long time, slid easily off Janessa's tongue.

Margarite swallowed and pointed at a pitcher of water and a cup.

Janessa filled the cup and held it to the other woman's lips. "Better?"

Margarite nodded. "Yes. I thought I was dead when he was squeezing my throat. I couldn't react, couldn't scream, and couldn't breathe."

"It's over, Mags. You're safe now. Potts has some explaining to do. But we'll talk about that later when you're discharged. Did Dr. Lenno say when you can get out of here?"

Margarite motioned for another sip of water. "Tomorrow. He says to stay home and rest for a day or two then I can return to work."

"Not nights. I don't care what Potts says. You're not working nights. I'll switch shifts too and work with you. I won't let her put you in jeopardy again. She knows there's a killer on the loose. Maybe that's her goal, to leave you alone and vulnerable."

There was a noise at the door. Both women looked up. Carla Potts stood there; hands on her hips as a means to intimidate. She was breathing heavily as if she'd run up the stairs and into the room. She was silent and neither Margarite nor Janessa initiated any conversation. Finally, the big woman everyone called the *Amazon*, moved into the room and stood at the end of the bed. Her green eyes were trained on Janessa. "Williams, you *will* work your usual eight-hour day shift. There is no question of you joining Nurse Barrett on nights. That's not going to happen. Have I made myself clear?"

"Perfectly," Janessa sneered. "I don't know why it's so important to you that Margarite work nights. She's in danger from an unknown attacker. The fact that she looks just like the dead woman, April Hill, hasn't gone unnoticed. There's a connection that has put her life in danger. I will not stand by while she's stalked and killed."

Carla smiled and moved closer to Janessa. "Nothing you can do about it, Williams. I call the shots around here, not you." She looked away from Janessa. "Margarite, Dr. Lenno says he's discharging you tomorrow. I expect to see you back here the next night to work from 7 PM to 7 AM. Understand?"

Margarite didn't speak. She looked at Janessa, her eyes filled with fear. "In your dreams, Potts." Janessa said. "There's no reason for her to be here at night after this attack. That is unless you have a motive other than meanness. Maybe you *are* her attacker and you want another chance. Is that it? Do you want her here to make sure the next time you kill her?"

Carla Potts sputtered. Janessa imagined she saw flames shooting out of the woman's ears. The thought made her giggle.

"You think this is funny, Williams? You'd better start taking me seriously. I'm not playing games with you and Barrett. She'll return to work on the night shift and you won't. You have no choice. I'm the supervisor and what I say goes. Is that clear?"

"Clear as mud, Carla. We'll see how far you get with your vendetta. I know why you're doing this, but you won't get away with it. If I were you, I'd change my stance or suffer the consequences. Is *that* clear?"

Carla gave a belly laugh that made her entire body jiggle. "Consequences from who? You? Or do you plan to go to HR and spill your nonsense to Bill? I seriously doubt that he'll listen to anything you have to say. He'd just as soon fire you as look at you. So run to him and do your worst. If you dare."

Janessa huffed. "You'd have to pay me more than I make before I'd go running to him. He's so ineffectual he wouldn't do anything anyway. No, Carla, other people will listen to me. I don't need to run to someone who's an even bigger bully than you."

"Gonna take your case to your daddy?" Carla taunted. "That won't get you anywhere either. He needs to start looking out for his job instead of bailing you out of your messes. And if you think Becca Doane will help you out, think again. She has no more use for you than I do. So, oops, out of options. You'll live with my decisions because you have no choice. If I say Barrett works nights, then she works nights."

Carla Potts hefted her bulk out of the door. Margarite began to cry, but Janessa was more determined than ever to stop Carla's bullying. She knew she was doing this because it was the only way she could get to Janessa. But this time it wouldn't work. She had an ace up her sleeve. The only problem was that she didn't know if she could contact him in time to prevent another attack on Margarite. All she could do was try.

Janessa patted Margarite's arm and made small soothing sounds. "What are we going to do, Janessa? I'm scared. I can't go back on nights." Margarite cried.

"Don't worry, I have a plan, and Carla won't be able to stop it once I set things in motion."

Margarite sniffed. "What's your plan, Janessa?"

"It's probably better if you don't know in case it doesn't work. But if I'm successful, not only will she leave you alone, but she'll also get out of my face. I'm going to go now. I can't put my plan in motion unless I get going. I have phone calls to make. The detectives are still here. I'll talk to Lance and Pete before I leave. That way I can make sure you have protection. We don't want a repeat of what happened earlier." Janessa smiled at Margarite and left the room.

Lance and Pete were still interviewing Franklin. She didn't want to leave until she'd spoken to one or the other of the detectives. She shuddered at the thought of leaving Margarite alone in the room with no one to monitor who came and went from the room. When Pete looked up and saw Janessa hovering in the doorway, he said something to Lance and left his chair.

"What's going on? Is Margarite okay?"

"She's doing as well as can be expected under the circumstances. I need to leave for a while, and I wanted you and Lance to know. Margarite is alone right now so you might want to post a policeman in her room. I don't think it's a good idea for her to be alone with anyone right now." She took a deep breath. "Especially Carla Potts."

Pete stared at her and stroked his chin. "Do you think she had something to do with this attack?"

"Anything is possible," Janessa said. "We can't be too careful. The next time whoever attacked Margarite might succeed."

Pete shook his head. "Don't even think it. I'll have one of the officers stand guard. Let me know when you get back."

Janessa smiled, waited until an officer stood outside Margarite's door, then left. She had a call to make and she couldn't do that in the hospital. She saw that Carla Potts was still talking to Margarite's temporary replacement, so she strode out the door and got onto the elevator. The drive to her house didn't take long. Her little dog, Brutus was waiting for her when she let herself inside. After replenishing his water, followed by doggy kisses and a quick trip to the back yard, she sat on her sofa and dialed a number she knew well.

Thirty minutes later she patted Brutus' head. She grabbed her keys, and headed out to her car. After climbing into her Mini Cooper, she started it up and headed back to the hospital. She pulled into the parking lot and then checked her watch. Midnight. She had to be at work at 7 am, but she'd resigned herself to getting little sleep. The important thing was that Margarite was protected from whoever was trying to kill her.

Janessa rode the elevator to the Critical Care Unit. When she walked through the doors, Barbara Cleason, Margarite's replacement, was the only person she saw. There was no sign of Carla Potts. She figured that would change shortly. She expected her to come charging through the door at any moment. By now she should have gotten a phone call. When she walked into Margarite's room, she saw that Pete was with her. The murmur of their voices reached Janessa as she walked into the room. She smiled at the couple. Pete was rubbing Margarite's hand as he bent over the bed and placed light kisses on her forehead.

Right on cue, Janessa heard the swish of the doors opening into the Critical Care Unit. Carla Potts stomped into Margarite's room. Janessa smiled at her. Carla pointed a finger in her direction. The supervisor's face was bright red. "Williams! What did you do?"

Chapter Thirteen

Janessa's grin widened. "Why Carla, how nice of you to join us." She glanced at Pete who'd straightened up to his full six-foot-four height. He looked so intimidating that Carla backed toward the door. "I made a couple of calls, but I haven't had a chance to tell Margarite and Pete the good news. You're just in time to hear," Janessa said.

She turned toward the couple and smiled, ignoring Carla Potts, who was making strangled noises in her throat. Janessa turned to stare at her, worried she was having a stroke. When she was sure Carla was okay, she moved closer to her friends. "Margarite, you don't have to worry about working nights anytime soon. You will take time off and stay with your parents. They'll be here to pick you up in the morning as soon as you're discharged. Carla has been told to find a replacement to work your night shift. When you're ready to return to work, it will be on days, with me."

Carla pointed at Janessa. She was still at a loss for words. "You, you..."

"I know. Isn't it great? Leo Scutterby agreed when I told him what happened to Margarite. He said he would call you and Ms. Doane and arrange for Margarite to take sick days and recover. He felt that because the police and I agreed that her life is in danger, she needs to be with other nurses on the day shift. He also agreed that Margarite and I should work together. We can be each other's backup. Isn't that fantastic?"

Carla waved her hand in the air. The strangled sound emitted from her again as she turned on her heel and marched out of the room. The three people in the room could hear her angry muttering but couldn't make out the words.

"Wow," Margarite croaked.

"When I left here, I called Leo and told him everything. He agreed. I explained about April Hill, and that someone had killed her, and that the same person had attempted to kill you earlier tonight. I also told him that the police have no idea who killed April or who attacked you, but that we have detectives checking on the situation. Nobody's gonna hurt you. Leo agreed to make phone calls to arrange for you to get time off, and you no longer have to work nights unless you want to. I told him you didn't. I also told him about my suspicions about Carla Potts, although I can't prove anything, but we do have help. He says we should let him know if we need anything else. He'll do whatever is necessary."

Janessa was startled when Pete shifted his position. She was so focused on Marguerite and telling her what she had accomplished, she forgot Pete was in the room. "When you say help, I assume you mean the police. I hate to think that you've pulled somebody else into a police investigation; a murder investigation."

For a minute, Janessa felt guilty for keeping secrets from the detectives, however, what they didn't know couldn't hurt them. She gave Pete a faint smile, looked directly into his eyes, and lied through her teeth. "No, Pete, there's no way we would keep anything from the police. After all, we need you. You came quickly tonight when Marguerite was attacked. I have to be certain you're there when we need you again. So no, I wouldn't keep things from you." Pete sank into his chair, but he continued to look at her. When he looked away, Janessa sighed with relief, then unfurled her crossed fingers.

She looked down at Marguerite, who gave the barest hint of a wink. Marguerite knew they were keeping things from the police, but it couldn't be helped. The faster they figured things out, the better. The police had to wait for tests results and reports. That took more time than they had. Janessa knew they had to call Charlie Piper, Marguerite's cousin, to find out if he had any new information about Marguerite's birth family. Who was Carla Potts? What was her relationship to Marguerite? What was her relationship with April Hill? There had to be a connection. They resembled each other. Although Carla's looks were faded, she still looked like April Hill, and April was dead. Carla also bore a faint resemblance to Marguerite. There was a family connection among the three women and Janessa planned to find out what and why someone killed April. Was it to keep her quiet? To keep her from telling Marguerite her real identity? The only way she could make sure that Marguerite was safe was to solve the mystery of the birth family and April's murder. If they could figure out the who, and why, then they could stop the murderer before anyone else got hurt or killed.

"Let me know if you need anything, Margarite. Relax with your family for the next few days. You need to get away from the stress of this place." Janessa looked around the room, her thoughts tumbling over each other. She looked back at Pete and Margarite. "I have to go now. I still have to work my shift in the morning. I need to be up at six am. Call me when you get to your parent's house." She leaned down, hugged Margarite, and waved to Pete as she left the room. Carla was outside the door, waiting to pounce.

"Don't think this is over. You think you've won, but I'm not done with you yet. You might have Leo Scutterby on your side, but I have other weapons I can use against you," Carla said. Her teeth were clenched and nearly as tight as her hands which were fisted at her side.

Janessa laughed. She knew she was antagonizing Carla further, but she couldn't seem to help herself. "Are you threatening me, Carla? There's a detective in the room with Margarite and I'm sure he'd be happy to hear your veiled threats."

"You'll see. You'll get what you deserve. Soon. And so will your whiney friend in there." Carla said as she stomped to the door. "Too bad she lived."

The next few days dragged for Janessa. Although she spoke to Margarite on the phone every day, it wasn't the same. By the time the weekend came, she'd cleaned her house from top to bottom, wishing that Margarite was there so they could discuss what happened to her and what their next move would be. Janessa was mopping the bathroom floor for the third time when her cell phone rang. She grabbed it off the counter.

"This is Janessa."

"I would hope so. I didn't think you'd have someone else there to answer your phone."

"Margarite! Is everything okay? How are you feeling?"

"Good grief. You'd never know that you just talked to me yesterday. I wanted to give you a heads up that I'm coming home this afternoon. I'll send you a text when I get there."

"How? I mean who's bringing you? Your car is here in Ashton."

"My brother says he can bring me. I love my family and it's been great being here, but I'm over all the hovering and pampering. I need to come back so we can figure out our next move."

Janessa sighed. She was relieved that Margarite was okay, but she was reluctant to drag her back into the investigation and put her at risk again. She also had no plans to tell her what Carla Potts said the night Margarite was attacked. "Are you sure you want to continue with this?"

"The investigation? How can you ask? I want to catch this person more than ever. I need to know who tried to kill me. Has it been quiet since I've been gone?"

"Too quiet. Even Brutus goes to the door and whines. I think he's looking for you."

Margarite laughed. "Either that or he has to go potty."

"That too, but we've both missed you. What time do you plan to be back here?" Janessa heard Margarite say something. Her voice was muffled as if she had her hand over the phone.

"I should be there about 2 o'clock. I'll text you when I get close. See you later."

Janessa clicked off the phone, picked up Brutus and twirled around the room. "Our buddy is coming home." She looked him in the eye. "Doesn't that make you happy?"

Brutus responded with a couple of licks to her cheek. She set him down on the floor and he immediately made a beeline for the back door. "So that's why you were dancing around. Margarite was right. You need to go." She laughed then opened the door for the little dog. He ran around in a circle once he was outside, until he found the right spot for his business. Janessa shivered in the chill, autumn air. She'd have to find her jacket before she went over to Margarite's apartment. The weather was much cooler than it had been a week ago. Leaves were falling off the trees. *I hope we find out who killed April before winter comes. Bad things happen in the dark, cold winter.* She shivered again then opened the door for Brutus.

Shortly before 2 o'clock, Janessa's phone chimed with a text. "She's home Brutus. I'm going to go over to Auntie Mag's house.," she said as she pulled on her jacket. The little dog ran to the door. "Not this time sweetie. Next time you can go." Janessa shut the door quickly. She hated his pitiful whine.

Janessa knocked on the apartment door. When it opened Margarite was standing there. Janessa folded her in her arms for a long hug, then stepped back to look at her. She studied her face and tilted her head from side to side to look at her neck. There were still faint marks from her attack. "You look good."

"Thank you. I feel much better."

"You sound like your old self as well. The other night I could barely hear you when you talked. He or she did a number on your neck and throat but thank God it wasn't worse." Janessa stepped away from Margarite and entered the apartment. A tall, lanky man sauntered into the room. "Charlie, it's so nice to see you again." Janessa reached up and gave him a hug.

"It's Trent now. I prefer my given name of Trent."

She was surprised. She and Margarite exchanged a glance. As long as she had known Margarite's brother, he'd been called Charlie. "If you don't mind my asking, why the change?"

He laughed and walked over to the brown leather recliner and sat down. "It's a long story, but let's just say that although Cousin Charlie is great, it's time I assumed my own identity instead of following him around like I did when I was a little kid. My full name is Trenton Charles Barrett. Now that I'm an adult it's time I use that name. My middle name is Charles so that part of me is still there, but for now, everyone calls me Trent."

"I see." Janessa sat on the sofa across from him, Margarite followed. "I don't see you that often, but I guess I can adjust to it. It's a nice name." She grinned at him.

"Thanks, Janessa." He got to his feet and held out his hand to his sister. When she stood, he pulled her into a tight hug. "I need to hit the road, Sis. Take care of yourself. Anyone else hurts you, call me. I'll take care of them. Better yet, call that absent boyfriend of yours and make him go after them. He *is* a detective."

Margarite pushed him away and laughed. "I love you Trent, now get your butt out of here. The drive to Bentor will take at least two hours and it gets dark earlier now."

After her brother left, Margarite asked Janessa, "Would you like tea? I could use another cup." She made her way to the kitchen. "By the way, where is Brutus? I thought you would bring him with you."

"Believe me, he wanted to come. But I figured that we wouldn't get any work done with him prancing around trying to get your attention." Margarite finished putting the kettle on the stove and turned to look at her.

"Okay, what did you find out while I was gone?" Margarite asked.

"We have to call your cousin Charlie and find out what he's discovered. There's got to be something. There's a reason Potts is after you to do nights. I don't know if she killed April or if she's the one who attacked you. If we can get more information about your birth family then perhaps, we'll know what her motives are and what she stands to gain by eliminating you. So, in a little while, we'll call and see what new information he has, if any. I have a gut feeling the killer is going to strike again. We need all the information we can get.

Chapter Fourteen

"Charlie's not answering," Janessa said as she turned off her cell phone. "I'll call him a little later. In the meantime, let's see who we have for suspects. Do you still have the board we set up when Lara was killed? Or do we need to go back to pen and paper?"

Margarite stood and walked down the hall to her bedroom. "Of course, we still have it. After all, you never know when we're going to stumble over a dead body." She smiled as she placed the easel-like board on the table. It was small enough to carry around but still had enough space to hold everything the women wanted to put on it.

"This is perfect," Janessa said, smiling back at Margarite. "Unless we get more than a dozen suspects, we should easily fit everyone on here. Let's list them. She wrote a number one on the board with the marker Margarite handed her. "First, we have Carla Potts. After your attack, she became my number one suspect. Her actions that night were very suspicious. We can't verify her whereabouts. She's also big. With her Amazonian proportions, she could be mistaken for a man in the dark. Next, we have Franklin Stevens. He was roaming around the unit, and we had no idea what he was doing there. He was told to stay away from there. He seems nice enough, but creepy. He's always around where he shouldn't be."

"Also, he lied to me and said he had permission to work in the Unit."

"Yes," Janessa said writing his name on the board. "And he doesn't work nights. I talked to Griff about it, and he said that not only didn't he permit Franklin to be there, but he was supposed to be on the day shift."

Margarite got up and fixed them both another cup of tea. "Do we have anyone else?" she asked.

"We do. I'm putting Bully Bill on the list as well. Although he's slow-moving because of his bulk he could have grabbed and choked you."

"But wait. He wasn't there was he?"

"He was. I heard Carla tell Barbara Cleason, the maternity nurse, that she was going to his office to let him know what was happening. I don't know if she spoke to him again after Leo's phone call to her or not. I know he was going to call Bully Bill first about your work schedule and as he put it, 'suggest' you work days with me and that they were to keep you off of nights, so I know he was there long enough. He could be the one who attacked you."

"Anyone else?" Margarite asked.

"Yes. I'm going to add Barbara Cleason to the list. She was over in the Maternity unit, but they had no patients. She's on the small side, but you were taken unaware, and she could have the upper body strength to strangle you."

"What would be her motive? She and I have always been friendly. We've worked together without any problems."

Janessa continued to write on the board. "That's a good question, but I'll leave her on the board until we eliminate people. And last but not least, although I'd hate to think he was culpable, is Griff Lewis."

"Griff? You can't be serious. He's the most mild-mannered person I've ever met. Why would he attack me? He's been watching out for me. Right?"

Janessa stopped the marker in mid-air. "You're right, he seems like a nice guy, and he said he was watching out for you, but was he? Besides, you've heard about those serial killers in the movies? The neighbors always say what quiet, unassuming people they were. Then they turn out to have killed 10 people. He had the opportunity. I don't know the motive. He was working at Ashton when April was killed. And," Janessa paused and looked directly at Margarite, "For a person who runs several departments, he spends too much time on the Critical Care Unit."

"I know, but..."

Janessa continued writing on the board. "Think about it. How much do we know about him and Franklin Stevens? They both started work at the same time. We don't know much about their backgrounds. We will though. I spoke to Charlie while you were at your parent's house. I told him everything I knew about the two men. He's going to look into them and, he's also going to do a deep dive into Carla Potts."

Margarite folded her arms across her chest and shook her head. "Now there's a likely suspect. That woman is insane and plain mean. If anyone has the nerve to do away with someone, she does. I don't trust her at all. She's big enough to strangle me and you too."

Janessa stifled a laugh. "Good point. I also think she has the best motive. Number one, she hates us, me in particular. She had means. She's big and strong enough to choke a woman your size. You're no dainty flower, but she's twice your size. She also had the opportunity. No one was around when you were attacked; she came huffing and puffing onto the Unit shortly after. And another thing is that she came out of the emergency room doors when I found April's body."

Janessa saw Margarite shiver and then grimace. "I went to get her that morning, but she was hovering in the emergency department when I found her. The thought of Carla Potts being that close to me gives me the creeps. So, is that it? Is our list complete?"

"As of right now, it is," Janessa said, standing back to look at her handiwork. "Now, let's relax for the rest of the weekend. I'm scheduled to do Safety rounds on Monday afternoon. It's such a joy. It's my favorite thing to do."

"Stop telling fibs. You hate it as much as I do. Who are you doing it with and where are you going?"

"My email said I'm with Rosa Jenkins and Griff of course. We get to go to the pharmacy and the boiler room. I'm not thrilled about visiting the boiler room, but at least I'll see Paulie while we're in the pharmacy."

"I wouldn't be too thrilled about being with a potential murderer either."

Janessa sighed, "There is that aspect of the whole thing. We don't know what Griff Lewis is capable of or even who he is. Sometimes a person's actions aren't a true sign of who the person is or what dark thoughts lurk in their mind."

"I guess it could be worse. You could be doing safety checks with Carla Potts."

Janessa clapped her hand to her forehead. "Spare me, please. Okay, we have one more day of freedom. I need to get home and show Brutus some love. I'll talk to you tomorrow. If anything comes to mind about the case, call me."

The girls hugged, and then Janessa walked out to the visitor's parking space she'd snagged in front of Margarite's apartment building. She climbed into her Mini Cooper thankful she lived only a few blocks away. Because the town was so small, with a population of under 3,400 people, there was little traffic. During tourist season in the summer and at the height of ski season that number swelled to triple the size or more. That also meant more injuries and ill people were streaming into Ashton Community Hospital. One never knew who would come into the hospital for treatment. Most of the people were nice tourists, although some were a little shady. For a few seconds Janessa wondered if there had been any suspicious tourists around when April was killed.

Janessa parked in the driveway of her small ranch house. Her Jack Russell terrier, Brutus, was looking out the window, his tail wagging a mile a minute. Her neighbor Gladys Ketchum was at her window. She must have been waiting, because before Janessa could get into her house the woman opened her door. "I noticed the police were here the other day. Are you in trouble again?"

"No, Mrs. Ketchum, I'm not. My boyfriend is one "of the detectives. He was here for a short visit." Janessa turned her back on the gossiping neighbor and walked to her front door. As soon as she opened it, Brutus jumped as high as he could trying to get into her arms. "I'm excited to see you too my little man. After you go out and take care of business, we'll walk down to the Barkery for a treat. As she talked, Janessa walked toward the back door where she could let Brutus out into the fenced area. At the word "treat," his little body wiggled all over. She was almost sure he'd done a happy dance. She noticed that the curtain at Mrs. Ketchum's kitchen window was moving as if it had been pulled back then dropped back down. *She's so nosy. Nothing going on here except a dog going potty. I hope she's satisfied with her voyeurism.*

The day was warmer now than it had been earlier. There was a light breeze and plenty of sun. The leaves were falling steadily despite not having much foliage this year. There were places where it was very colorful, but it was dry in Ashton and the surrounding areas. There was a red flag warning throughout the county and the neighboring states, signaling no burning of any kind. Janessa decided to enjoy the good weather despite the dryness and the dust kicking around and mixing with the leaves. "I would have asked Margarite to join us, Brutus, but she just got home. She needs to rest and get ready for work on Monday," Janessa picked up the little dog and walked into the Barkery, a store specializing in treats for dogs, like Brutus' favorite, peanut butter biscuits. Joyce, the owner, used only organic ingredients with no preservatives that could make a dog sick.

Janessa put Brutus on the floor but kept him on his leash. It was long enough so that he could go to the end of the counter and greet his favorite server. Joyce bent down to doggie level and seemed happy to be the recipient of Brutus kisses. In return, he was given a peanut butter dog biscuit. He lay on the floor at Janessa's feet and happily munched his treat.

Joyce glanced around the room. When she saw that they were alone she said to Janessa, "I heard about what happened to Margarite. How is she doing?"

Janessa smiled at the older woman. "She's better. She'll be back to work on Monday. I'll tell her you asked about her."

Joyce nodded. "There are some real sickos out there. I hope the police get the guy soon. You can't trust anyone these days. When you get attacked in your own hospital, it's bad. This town is so small, you'd think we wouldn't have much crime, but it's everywhere these days. What else can I get for our little sweetie?" She looked down at Brutus and smiled. He seemed content to lick crumbs off his paws and the floor. Joyce gave him a pat on the head and then looked expectantly at Janessa. After procuring a small bag of treats for the dog, Janessa and Brutus walked home at a leisurely pace. The rest of the day was uneventful, so the two of them went to bed after an early dinner.

Monday morning dawned clear and crisp. Janessa looked at the sky on her way to her car and decided it was still too early for snow. Good thing too. She and Brutus weren't fans of the white stuff. She drove a short distance to the doggie daycare. Brutus was in a hurry to get out. She'd barely stopped the car when he started whining and jumping around, eager to see his friends, a Dalmatian named Sid and a terrier named Ponty.

After settling Brutus with his doggy friends, Janessa drove to Margarite's apartment building. She wanted her friend close so she'd be safe, so she'd told her they would go to work in Janessa's car. Margarite was waiting outside. She had on a light green fleece jacket she had pulled tight. She climbed in Janessa's car, which was warm from being driven to the town.

"Heat! That feels so good. It's so cold out. Why, oh why, don't I live in the south?"

"You'd hate it. What are you going to do when winter comes?"

"Freeze probably. When are you going to get a bigger car? If a squirrel runs into this one, it will be totaled."

"Very funny. It's not that small. I see you're in good spirits and ready to go this morning. Don't forget I have Safety rounds this afternoon. I'll tell Paulie, hi for you. I'm going to see if I can get Griff to talk about his life. Maybe I'll learn something about him so we can eliminate him as a suspect. Although, there's something odd about him."

Margarite turned in her seat to face Janessa who started driving toward the hospital as soon as Margarite fastened her seat belt. "Please be careful. We don't know who we're dealing with. He might be as nice as he seems but on the other hand..."

"I know," Janessa said, gripping the steering wheel, "he could be a killer. Don't worry, it's not like we'll be alone in the boiler room. Rosa Jenkins will be with us. He wouldn't dare try anything. I think I'm safe, for today anyway."

Chapter Fifteen

At one o'clock, Janessa took the elevator to the ground floor where Griff Lewis' office was located. She was the first one there, so she decided to snoop through the papers on his desk. She didn't find much information; she also didn't hear him come into the room.

"Find what you were looking for?" Griff asked. He was smiling.

Janessa jumped. "I didn't hear you. You scared me half to death." *Poor choice of words, Williams.* She grimaced and looked at him, noticing his smile didn't reach his eyes. His eyes seemed to be looking past her, into her soul. "Is Rosa coming with us?"

"She should be here any minute. Ah, here she is now. We can get started," Griff said, handing each woman a clip board and taking one himself. "We'll go to the pharmacy first. Look for any medications that are outdated or any open vials. Make sure any used vials are in the proper container. Not too long ago someone found two insulin vials in the trash can in the porter's closet off the emergency department."

Janessa was surprised he knew about the incident. It had happened before Griff started working at Ashton. "I remember that incident. I was working in the emergency department at the time. One of the housekeepers found them. Do you know how they got there? I never heard the result of that incident."

Griff smiled a genuine smile. "According to the housekeeper who told me about it, a nurse stole the vials. It turns out her mother is a diabetic and couldn't afford her medication."

Rosa stopped walking. "I heard about that. The hospital found a program for the mom so she could get her insulin at a steep discount. The nurse was put on probation and isn't allowed near any meds. That was the condition of her probation. If she violates that the hospital will press charges, and she'll go to jail. She's been doing well, so she was just desperate to take care of her mother."

Janessa stopped as well. "I'm glad she was given a chance to redeem herself. I'd hate to see her career go down the drain for one bad choice." *Hmmm, that's not the story I heard about those vials. I wonder who twisted things around to take the spotlight off Emily? It makes for a nice feel-good story. Too bad it's not true.*

Griff started walking toward the pharmacy. "We all make bad choices occasionally. Unfortunately, not all of us get a second chance. The first choice sometimes can have deadly consequences. Right?"

Janessa shuddered, but both women nodded their agreement. When they got to the pharmacy, Paulie Standard was working. He grinned when he saw Janessa. "Safety rounds, eh? Guess I better be on my toes. Sleuth Janessa is on the case."

She smiled back at Paulie. "Just Nurse Williams, that's it. Although I will be looking to see if everything is in order in this pharmacy. You know the usual, outdated medications or half-empty vials that aren't stored properly."

Janessa looked around and noted Griff's frown. Rosa was busy inspecting packages on one of the shelves, so she got to work. She opened the refrigerator to make sure the medications in there were labeled correctly. She checked the thermometer to see if it was at the correct temperature. Everything seemed okay, so she closed the door and smiled at Paulie. "The fridge looks good, Paulie. It's nice and clean, nothing is out of date, and nothing is in there that shouldn't be, including your lunch."

Rosa laughed and Paulie's face turned bright red. "I haven't done that since I first started working here over ten years ago. I learned my lesson in a hurry."

Griff joined in the laughter. "Tell me you didn't really store your lunch in the refrigerator with all the vaccines and other refrigerated medications. What were you thinking?"

"Way to go, Janessa. Rat me out and make me look like a fool. Thanks. I thought you were my good friend."

"I'm sorry, Paulie. It was a rookie mistake that anyone could have made. You were new and didn't know there were two refrigerators; one in the other room for food and this one in here for medications. I'm simply happy the Joint Commission wasn't inspecting that week. That would have been a disaster."

"I was so embarrassed. But hey, I lived through it and I'm a better man for having been through that experience. I must have been forgiven because the powers that be let me run the place now."

"That's true," Griff said. "Okay, I think we're finished here. Paulie, you're all set. I didn't find any problems or deficits. How about you ladies?"

Janessa and Rosa agreed with Griff and followed him out of the pharmacy door after saying goodbye to Paulie. Just as they began walking toward the boiler room, Rosa's Calltec alarm buzzed. She turned away and pushed the button to answer the call. Janessa and Griff could clearly hear the speaker. "Rosa," the disembodied voice said, "I know you're on safety rounds, but we need you in the Emergency Department. We have a six-car pile-up with multiple injuries coming. The first ambulance will be here in about ten minutes."

"I'm on my way."

Rosa turned to Griff and Janessa. "Sorry. I have to go."

"We understand. I told you when you signed up for this session that if you had to leave, it would be all right. Go. Save lives. Janessa and I can finish this up. The boiler room won't take that long, right, Janessa?"

"Right." She smiled at Rosa then gestured that she should hurry toward the elevator. Janessa turned back to look at Griff. "I'm ready when you are. I don't think I've ever been in the boiler room. What will we be looking for?"

"We need to check the gauges and make sure they're on the right settings. You might say that all the inner workings of the hospital are in that room. If it doesn't run correctly, the hospital could shut down."

Janessa began walking toward the small room that housed the mechanics of the hospital. "We certainly can't let that happen, can we?"

When she and Griff walked into the room, Janessa looked around, partly curious, partly nervous to be alone with the man she knew so little about. She spotted a chair in one corner with a small table in front of it. "What are...?" she began but stopped talking. Griff was close, too close.

"It's just the two of us, now," he said quietly as he pulled the heavy door closed behind them.

Janessa backed as far away from Griff as she could get. She could feel the control panel at her back. She fumbled behind her hoping there would be some kind of weapon she could use. Nothing. She could feel her breathing increase as her panic level rose. She forced herself to remain calm and breathe slowly. "What is it that we need to look for while we're in here?"

Griff leaned over her so that she was trapped between his arms. "Turn around and look at the panel, and I'll explain it to you." She slowly turned, but his arms were still around her, making it harder for her to control her fear.

Suddenly she could hear Lance's voice so clearly it was as if he was in the room with them. His voice was soft and low, bringing back memories of her self-defense class. Just as she was prepared to use a move to immobilize him, Griff stepped back. "See these gauges," he asked pointing to the panel above her head. "These are the readings that we have to look at. You see that they are within a range, so that if a gauge isn't exactly where it should be, it shouldn't matter as long as it's within the range. We have a problem if anything is wildly outside of the normal area. Do you see what I mean? You need to compare the readings to those on the chart on your right."

Janessa nodded, then stepped away and went off to the side. She was feeling more in control now that he had backed off. "Yes, I understand. Does that mean that if only one gauge is off, we have a problem?"

Griff laughed. "Good question. It depends on which gauge it is. Some have more importance than others." He pointed to several at the top of the panel. Someone always has to be alerted if any of these are off. The lower ones are important too, but the top ones are more fine-tuned than the others."

"I think I see what you mean. I see the chart you mentioned. How often do you check?"

"At least once a day. I spend a lot of time here monitoring things when I have enough staff to deal with any other problems the department has. If I'm short-staffed then I'll check in here, but I'm only in here long enough to do a quick check."

"That seems like a lot of work. Is anyone else trained to do this job?"

"Of course. You should always have a backup plan," he said, his eyes were boring into hers.

Janessa felt uncomfortable again. "Is that all? she asked as she handed him the clipboard.

"That's it for today. Thank you, Nurse Williams, for coming on safety rounds with me today. Almost everyone does their best to try and avoid it, but it's mandatory twice a year for all staff."

She walked to the door, reached for the handle and pulled it open. "How well I know. This is my last set of rounds for this year anyway."

She stepped out into the hallway, Griff close behind her. "Do you know when Ms. Barrett is due for rounds?"

Janessa couldn't speak for a few seconds. She had to remind herself to take a breath. "Why would you ask me that?" She turned and was facing Griff. Her initial relief at being out of the boiler room faded. Fear clawed at her, fear for Margarite.

He held up his hands in mock surrender. "No reason. Just making conversation. I like her and I want to make sure she's safe. I meant no harm."

The security Janessa was beginning to feel evaporated quickly. She didn't trust this man. After all, they knew very little about him and his background. For all she knew she might have spent the last hour with a cold-blooded killer. His questions about Margarite heightened her suspicions. "I don't know when she has rounds but rest assured that she will be protected. She works the day shift now so there are plenty of people around. Whenever she does have to do safety rounds, at least she'll be inspecting another department. She won't have to go to the boiler room." *And she won't have to be alone with you.* "I have to get back to the unit. Thank you for explaining everything to me about the hospital operations."

"You're welcome. I'll see you around the facility."

Was she imagining things, or did his words hold the hint of a threat? She made a mental note to talk to Pete and Lance about Griff. But first, she and Margarite needed to call Charlie and see if he'd found out more background on Franklin, Griff and Carla. Anyone of them seemed capable of murder. She shuddered to think that she was in a room in the lower confines of the hospital with a possible psychopath. One who might be looking to kill her best friend.

Janessa's breathing was ragged by the time she got back to the Critical Care Unit. She nearly ran to the nurse's station and flopped into a chair in front of the computers. She looked at Margarite, but didn't speak.

"Good grief, Janessa, was it that bad? You look like you've seen a ghost. Your face has very little color and that can't be good."

Janessa let out a breath. "It wasn't that bad unless you call being in a room in the bowels of the hospital with a man you think might be a murderer. No, it wasn't bad at all."

"Wow. You really think the killer might be Griff? Did he tip his hand and give you a clue that he might be the one who killed April and tried to kill me?"

Janessa shook her head. She didn't want to tell Margarite that Griff had been asking questions about her. "We need to call Charlie and see what he's found out about our three people of interest. He must have some information by now."

Margarite's eyes widened. "Now you're scaring me. Griff claimed he found me when he was making rounds, but what if he was the one trying to kill me? Oh yeah, I forgot to tell you. Charlie called. He couldn't reach you, so he called me. He says he has some information, but he didn't say who the information was about."

Chapter Sixteen

J anessa sat in the chair next to Margarite. "We have no way of proving anything right now. So, let's keep doing what we do best and let the chips fall where they will. You'll stay with me so that there won't be any more night shift attempts on your life. But, let me tell you the best part about today."

Margarite stared at her, a quizzical look on her face. "What?"

"I heard that the two insulin vials were from a nurse who stole the insulin for her diabetic mother. Instead of jail the hospital treated her compassionately and made sure she got treatment for her mother and put the nurse in a program for offenders who steal drugs."

"That's not true. We know that Emily was the one who stole the drugs."

Janessa sat straighter in the chair. "I think they put that story out to spare Leo, but what difference does it make that people know that his daughter stole the drugs. She's a convicted murderer now. But enough about that. Maybe we'll get lucky, and Charlie will have some information we can use to catch whoever murdered April Hill. I asked him to look into all three of our suspects. For the life of me I can't figure out who is most likely to be the murderer. They're all shady. Griff just scared the heck out of me."

Margarite looked horrified. "What did he do? Did he touch you or anything like that? We'll call Lance and Pete to come and arrest him."

"No, nothing like that. It's just that when we were in the boiler room, he was a little too close." Janessa explained that Rosa had to leave the safety tour when they were halfway through because of critical patients being admitted to the emergency department.

133

"I know. We might be getting one of the patients that was involved. She was being sent for a Cat Scan then on to X-Ray if the CT didn't show anything major that would send her for emergency surgery instead. She should be coming to us very soon."

"I figured we might have a patient. Anyway, let me finish telling you the rest of what happened before we get busy." Janessa told Margarite about the incident with Griff in the boiler room. Then she decided she'd better tell her that Griff was asking questions about her and what he wanted to know. Just as she finished, the double doors opened. Rosa the emergency room nurse, and an emergency room assistant came through with a gurney. A white-haired older woman lay motionless on the stretcher. Margarite and Janessa got up to help move the patient to an empty room. When she was settled, Janessa went to the nurse's station with Rosa to get a report on the patient's condition.

"Your patient," Rosa said, gesturing toward the door, "is Henrietta Lansing. She was in one of the cars in the accident. Most of the other patients had minor injuries, but she was in the first car, driving the one that was hit by the SUV. She has multiple fractures, involving her left arm and leg. The doctor who attended wanted her to be in the Critical Care Unit for a couple of days before she gets moved to the medical/surgical floor. She complained of chest pain, although he couldn't find anything other than bruised ribs and an area above her breasts that was bruised. Her cardiac enzymes were normal, and her electrocardiogram showed no changes. She was in last year for a minor surgical procedure so her EKG was fairly recent. The trauma might be from her air bags, which deployed. She's not very big so they could be responsible for the damage she suffered. Now, I'll collect my assistant and leave Henrietta in your capable hands." With a small wave, she and her assistant grabbed the now empty gurney, disappeared out of the door and headed toward the elevator.

"Thanks, Rosa," Janessa called as she followed her and stood in the doorway while Rosa and her assistant waited for the elevator.

"When you get a minute, you'll have to tell me how the rest of the safety tour went. I was kind of glad to leave. Griff gives me the creeps."

Rosa turned, grabbed the gurney and motioned for her assistant to follow before Janessa could ask her why she felt that way about Griff. Janessa entered the room where Henrietta lay in the bed. She was quiet but attempted a smile. Margarite was bustling around the room making sure the woman was comfortable. "I see that you have everything under control so I'm going to review the notes from the emergency department," Janessa said. " If we get any other calls to admit patients, I'll let you know. Otherwise take all the time you need with Henrietta. May I call you Henrietta?"

The woman nodded slightly then closed her eyes. Janessa took that as her cue to leave the room. She tiptoed to the door, stopped and looked at Margarite. "We'll talk later," she whispered. Once she got to the nurse's station Janessa sat down and looked over the papers Rosa had given her. Every treatment the patient had done was listed on the forms as well as her diagnosis. Janessa logged into her computer and accessed Henrietta's electronic medical records. The nurses were lucky that there were no other patients in the Critical Care Unit at that moment. They had discharged their last patient shortly before Margarite got the call that the Emergency department was sending someone up to them. It was quiet, but there were a couple more hours until the next shift came in to work. Janessa hoped that nothing happened to disturb that. She liked that she and Margarite could take turns and give the patient extra one-on-one care when she needed it the most. It was obvious she was in a lot of pain and that she was probably emotionally traumatized.

A few minutes later, Margarite came out of the room and sat down at the nurse's station. She made a few notes in Henrietta's medical record and sighed. "Poor woman. She said she was scared that she was going to die in the crash. I guess the other person rammed into the side of her car, Rosa's assistant said he didn't make it. The other cars involved were minor incidents."

Janessa shook her head. "That's a shame. Did she tell you who it was that didn't make it?"

"She wasn't sure, but I can make a good guess. She said it was a young man in his early twenties. I guess he was racing another car and never stopped at the intersection. Probably so he could get ahead of the other car. She wasn't sure of his name, but it sounded like Ben or Ted or something like that."

Janessa covered her mouth with her hand, her eyes wide with shock. "I bet it was Ted Rentham. He's twenty-two and he drives like a demon. He's always trying to race any car that stops next to him. His poor parents will be heartbroken. He was their only child."

Both nurses were deep in thought when the double doors into the Critical Care Unit opened. They turned to see Griff Lewis walking through the doors. "Griff. What a surprise. We weren't expecting you to come up to the floor this afternoon. Didn't you tell me you had a lot of paperwork to do relating to our findings during the safety tour?"

"I did, but I needed a break. And I wanted to see how Ms. Barrett was doing. After you were nearly killed the other night, we can't be too careful."

Janessa and Margarite looked at each other before looking over at Griff. "I'm fine Griff," Margarite said. "Thank you for asking. I appreciate it. I'm also grateful you were in the right place at the right time when I needed you. Otherwise..." She couldn't finish the sentence. Janessa saw the sheen of unshed tears and put her arm around Margarite.

"I'm sorry, Ms. Barrett. I didn't mean to upset you. I just wanted to check and make sure that you were okay after everything that happened. I'll go now." He turned to leave the Critical Care Unit. The women looked at each other again, then eyed his departing figure.

"Do you buy that act?" Janessa asked, looking at Margarite.

"You think it was an act? Why would he do that?"

"He was fishing. I think he wanted to know if we have any clues about what happened. He might very well be the one responsible. I'm beginning to distrust him more and more. Especially after being alone with him in the boiler room. He was too close to me and asked too many questions about you. He's a stranger to you, right?"

Margarite grabbed a tissue from the box on the desk. She wiped her eyes, blinked twice then looked at Janessa. "I've known him as long as you have. Before he started working here, I had no idea who he was. He gives me the creeps. I didn't think about it before and he may have saved my life, but I don't trust him, and I definitely don't want to be alone with him."

"Me either. Rosa says he gives her the creeps, too," Janessa said as she stood. "I'm going to check on Henrietta. It's good that she's the only patient here at the moment. We can give her one on one care."

Janessa entered the room where Henritta was softly moaning in her sleep. She tried to roll over, but, stopped. Her sharp intake of breath told Vanessa it was too painful to move around much. The cast on her leg was also a deterrent. In a day or two Henrietta might be able to use the pulley suspended above the bed to pull herself up. Her eyes opened and she looked at Janessa. For a brief moment she seemed confused about where she was. She looked at her leg elevated slightly on a pillow, groaned and said, "The accident really happened, didn't it? I thought I was having a nightmare and that I was fine. Instead, I'm in a real-life nightmare."

Janessa moved closer to the bed. "I'm sorry this happened to you. How is your chest pain?"

"It feels sore, but the intense pressure with pain is gone. I think that's okay. Do you know how long I'll have this cast on?"

"Several weeks is the usual practice, but that's a question you need to ask your doctor. On a scale of one to ten, what is your pain level?" She saw a grimace flash across Henrietta's face.

"It's about a seven. A real throbbing, like an insistent toothache only more painful. How bad is my broken leg. I've never broken anything before."

"You have what's called a transverse fracture of the tib fib. That means the fracture wasn't an open fracture, so you didn't need surgery. Transverse means it's straight across the bones of your leg, the tibia and fibula. The emergency room doctor explained it to you, but I'm sure you were in too much pain and shock to understand what he was telling you. The Orthopedic doctor will be in to see you. She can tell you more and explain everything in more depth."

"Thank you," Henrietta said, sinking back onto the pillows with a sigh.

Janessa was pleased to see that Henrietta's breathing was no longer labored. "I'm going to see if it's time for you to have more medication for the pain. I'll be right back." Janessa left the room and sat in front of her computer, Henrietta's electronic medical record in front of her.

"How is she?" Margarite asked.

"She's about a seven on the pain scale. I don't want it to escalate, so if it's time, I'll give her something for the pain. She's been prescribed Tramadol for the first 24 hours then the doctor wants to switch to Ibuprofen to see how she tolerates the pain on that." Janessa removed the keys on a lanyard around her neck and selected the one to the medicine closet. "Will you get a set of vital signs on her while I get the medication?" She opened the medication room to access the automated medication dispenser.

Margarite left her chair. "Sure, no problem." She was back in a few minutes with the results. Janessa went to the patient's room and gave Henrietta the medication. She smiled at the elderly woman and patted her hand, then checked the IV that was in her arm. The fluid was nearly gone. "I'll check with the doctor to see if we can take this out." She motioned toward the intravenous line. That will be one less thing for you to worry about."

Henrietta offered a wan smile. "Thank you, nurse..., I'm sorry I've forgotten your name."

"It's Janessa. Try to rest. Let the medication do its work. If you need anything here is your call bell." She made sure it was clipped to the bed within easy reach. "Is there anything else you need? Margarite and I will be going off duty in a little while, but you'll be in good hands."

Henrietta nodded. "I'm fine. Thank you for everything. You and the red-haired nurse are great. I'm good now. How are the other people in the accident? The car that hit me came out of nowhere. Is everyone okay?"

Janessa decided it wasn't her place to tell Henrietta about the fatality. "I'm not sure. Other than the patients we get from there, the emergency department doesn't always tell us the outcomes. Try to rest." Janessa walked back to the nurse's station to see Carla Potts towering over Margarite. She had her hand raised as if she was about to hit the younger woman, who was shrinking back in her chair. "What is going on out here? I leave for two minutes and come out to find you brow beating Margarite. What is your problem?"

"I'm not browbeating her."

"It sure looked that way to me. Why are you standing over her with your hand raised?"

Carla's face flushed red. "I-I was just illustrating a point I was trying to make to Barrett."

Janessa was furious. She could see that Carla was intimidating Margarite, who was no shrinking violet. "And what would that point be, Carla?"

"The point that she only has a few more days on this shift then she'll be working nights again. And I'll be working with her."

Chapter Seventeen

Janessa moved closer to Carla and Margarite. "That's not going to happen. Now get away from her and go supervise somewhere else besides this unit."

"You will *not* talk to me that way," Carla said through clenched teeth.

"I just did. Go about your business Carla. Nothing to see here. In case you're interested the patient we have is doing as well as can be expected. She was just medicated and is resting comfortably. Anything else I can do for you?" The supervisor's mouth gaped open. She took one look at Janessa's face and backed away from the nurse's station without a word. She edged toward the patient's room.

When Carla found her voice, she was still edging toward the door. "I'll just go in and say hello to Mrs. Lansing."

Margarite started to speak, but Janessa held up her hand to stop her. "Not here. We'll be off shift in a few minutes. We'll talk when we leave. Come to my house We can talk there. We can also call Charlie to see what he's found. Now, we need to call the doctor and see if we can remove Mrs. Lansing's IV. She's sipping liquids and her pain has decreased."

Thirty minutes later Janessa and Margarite were done with Huddle. Their replacements were busy with their beginning routine. After they clocked out, the women walked to Janessa's car. She shivered in her light-weight jacket. "Time to break out the heavies," she said as she walked beside Margarite. "It's cold and it's not even winter yet. A week ago, we were wearing shorts and t-shirts."

Margarite burrowed into her jacket. "The joys of New England." She laughed. "And to think we chose to live here, so I guess we can't complain. As you told me, if we moved to a warmer climate we'd hate it."

"We can't complain, although spring and summer went by all too fast. And we had to end our warm weather by finding a dead body." The nurses arrived at Janessa's Mini Cooper. She unlocked the door. "I have to get Brutus from doggy daycare but that will be quick."

"You're the one who always finds the dead bodies. I just go along for the ride. Although this is one ride I'd rather not take."

They laughed. Despite the thoughts of a murdered woman racing through Janessa's mind, she remembered the past winter when the heater in Margarite's car broke down. She nearly had icicles on her red nose when she arrived at work one day, but she stubbornly refused to take the car to anyone, except her friend who lived nearby and was a mechanic. Thankfully he came home from his out-of-town trip a couple of days later. Despite the inconvenience of a broken car, they'd had fun until the warm weather came and with it the body of April Hill.

Janessa considered the puzzle of the dead woman as she drove to the doggy daycare to pick up Brutus. She mentally reviewed the facts that they'd discovered so far, but they weren't enough. Now someone was trying to kill Margarite. The way things were progressing they needed to find out who and why sooner rather than later. After the incident with Griff Lewis, he was high on the list of suspects. He had way too much interest in Margarite. It was creepy. As far as Carla was concerned, Janessa was trying to figure out why she was so keen on having Margarite work nights unless she was the killer and wanted her to be alone like the last time. Whoever it was almost succeeded in eliminating Margarite.

The only other suspect they had was Franklin Stevens and he'd hardly been around over the past week or two. What was he doing?

Was he who he said he was? Was he busy plotting his next move? So many questions with no answers. Janessa also thought about Lance and Pete. The two detectives knew the women were investigating, although they'd been told not to, but it seemed that the police moved at a snail's pace when Janessa thought they needed answers quickly, before someone succeeded in killing Margarite.

When she stopped in front of Nips and Yips. She could hear the yelps and barks as soon as she got out of her car. Brutus loved going there, which was a good thing, or Janessa wouldn't know what to do with him when she had to work. Because it was in the town of Ashton and was close to her home, it was the ideal setup. Margarite stayed in the car while Janessa walked to the door of the shop, opened it and went in. She could hear the commotion from the dogs who were playing in the back, which was fenced in so no one could escape when the front door was opened. Brutus was being chased by a Shi Zhu but stopped running when he spotted Janessa. He ran over and began barking and wiggling his butt. Although he loved playing with his friends, it was obvious he loved his mother more.

Janessa waited while Samantha, the owner of the doggy daycare, picked Brutus up and lifted him over the fence into her arms. Brutus immediately showered her with doggy kisses. "Thanks, Samantha. He's always so excited to be here. Aren't you little guy?" Brutus kissed her again. "I guess that's a yes."

The women laughed and headed to the front of the shop. Janessa always paid for the month, so she still had a couple of weeks before the bill was due. The peace of mind she felt when leaving Brutus there was well worth the price. She said goodbye to Samantha, then she and Brutus went to her car. After opening the back door of the car, she put Brutus in his dog restraint. She closed the back door, opened her own, and slid behind the steering wheel. Brutus yipped and wriggled. "Do you see your favorite aunt?" she asked as she turned to Margarite and smiled. The drive home was short. Janessa undid the dog restraint to let Brutus out. Shivering as she and Margarite walked to the door. *Definitely time to pull out the heavy coat. Winter is on its way.*

Margarite curled up on the sofa. She reached out to the small dog. "Come here, Brutus. Come and say a proper hello to Auntie Mags." He jumped onto the couch and into her arms. "Did you miss me? I know you did." The little dog covered her face with kisses before jumping down and running to the back door to be let out.

Janessa let him out into the fenced in backyard, then filled his water and food bowls.

"Do you want something to eat, Margarite? As soon as Brutus is done and back inside, we can make a snack, then we'll call Charlie. Hopefully he found something. Anything to let us know who these people are and what we need to look out for. I mean..." The doorbell chimed just as she walked to the back door to let Brutus in. "Will you see who's there, Margarite? If you don't know them, don't open the door."

When Brutus was ready to come inside. Janessa listened for a moment. She recognized the voices coming from her living room. The detectives were standing by the door. "Lance, Pete, what brings you two here?" She approached Lance and gave him a light kiss. Margarite and Pete separated as she turned around with Lance's arm still around her. She saw the men look at each other before Lance spoke.

"We wanted to check on Margarite and see how she's doing. When she wasn't at her place, we figured we'd check here. So, any news about the strangler?"

"You're asking us?" Margarite stuttered. "You two are the detectives. What have you discovered? Besides, you told us to stay out of your investigation."

Pete laughed. "That's never stopped you two before." He gasped when Margarite elbowed him in the ribs. "We wanted to know if you had more trouble. Has anyone approached you and seemed suspicious or overly concerned?"

"Just Griff Lewis." Janessa clapped her hand over her mouth. She hadn't intended to mention him to the detectives.

"What about him? Has he bothered either of you?"

Janessa watched the red seep into Lance's face. A glance at Pete confirmed that he felt the same building anger. "No, he didn't touch me, it was the way he's been acting and some things he said to me, to us."

"Tell me now." Lance's teeth were clenched so tight, Janessa had to strain to hear what he was saying. She hesitated, not wanting to throw around accusations. For all she knew Griff could be an innocent man who was genuinely concerned about Margarite. "What did he do? What did he say? Has he been harassing the two of you?"

She sighed and looked at Margarite who was white-faced, her breaths shallow. "I had to do Safety Rounds with him a couple of weeks ago. It was fine until Rosa, the Emergency Department nurse, was called back to her department. We'd finished inspecting the pharmacy by then, but we had to check out the boiler room."

"Boiler room?" Pete asked. "Is that usual?"

"Yes," Janessa said looking at him. "Every department gets a safety inspection so we can correct any problems before the Joint Commission comes to review."

"Joint Commission?" Lance asked. He looked confused by the name.

"Yes. It's the Joint Commission for Accreditation. If they ding us for too many things, we could be shut down. It would also affect the amount of money we get reimbursed by Medicare and Medicaid. Eventually we'd go belly up."

"Wow," Pete said. "That sounds pretty serious. I hope Ashton gets a good report. I'd hate to have to travel an hour to the nearest hospital."

Janessa smiled. "They give us time to correct any problems. They usually don't find many things wrong at Ashton. We have an excellent record. So, anyway, let me finish telling you about Griff." She told the detectives about her trip to the boiler room with Griff and how he'd gotten too close, almost blocking her way out. She told them about his remarks about Margarite and how he'd even arrived at the Critical Care Unit later to talk to Margarite. She looked at Pete and saw his hands clenched, the knuckles white. Looking back at Lance she saw the white line around his mouth. His mouth was pinched together, lips pulled thin. The detectives were furious, but more than that both of them seemed worried. *This is bad. I wish I hadn't told them.*

"I'm glad you told us. That's a good lead. We'll keep a close eye on him. I suppose you still have to deal with him when you work, right?"

Janessa nodded. She was worried the police would storm the hospital and arrest Griff only to find out he was innocent. She should have known better. Neither detective worked that way.

"Unfortunately, we don't have any concrete information to arrest Griff. We can watch him though. I want you to stay away from him as much as possible. If he continues to harass you, call us immediately. We'll deal with him. Understand?" His gaze encompassed both women.

Margarite answered. "Of course we understand. I for one don't want to put my life in any more jeopardy than it's in right now. If either Griff or Franklin acts out or does anything unusual, we'll call you right away."

"Franklin?" Pete asked. "Who's Franklin?"

"He's a fairly new housekeeper. He was acting really weird the night I was attacked." Margarite said.

"Explain weird," Pete said.

"Well," continued Margarite. "He wasn't supposed to be working on our unit, but he came there and was cleaning around the nurse's station. When I questioned him about it, he was belligerent and said he had been told to work there. Later, Janessa asked Griff about it and he denied giving Franklin permission to work in the Critical Care Unit. Franklin was told to stay away from the patient areas and work on the ground floor. He wasn't supposed to be working in the Critical Care Unit."

Janessa spoke up, "There are only administration offices on the floor he was assigned to clean. During the day there is office staff, but he had no business coming to our unit. He was concentrating on the nurse's station. One day he was there, and I caught him as he was about to dip his hand in Margarite's purse. He claimed he was cleaning, but denied touching anyone's belongings. The next thing we knew, Carla made him leave and go down to the ground floor to clean, although we hadn't reported him."

"So anyway, the night I was attacked," Margarite said, "I called Janessa and told her that Franklin was in our unit. He's creepy. I was uncomfortable because I was alone at that time. I called Griff. He dealt with the situation. As the department head, it's his responsibility to keep track of his employees."

"This Franklin seems a bit suspicious. He might just be a petty thief, but we can't take that chance. He could be our murderer trying to throw us off track by pretending to try to steal things. We'll check into him a little deeper. In the meantime, you ladies need to stop investigating." He stared at Janessa then looked over at Margarite. "I mean it. Someone could get hurt and I'd just as soon it wasn't either of you. It's bad enough that we have the head of maintenance trapping you in the boiler room," he said staring at Janessa. "Now you tell me one of the housekeepers is stalking you. Is there anything else we should know?"

Janessa hesitated, but she had a poor poker face. Her expression said it all. "Out with it. What else have you two been doing?"

"It's not us!" Janessa tried to lower her voice and moderate her tone, but she was annoyed that Lance was determined to blame her and Margarite for things beyond their control. "It's Carla Potts. She's determined to have Margarite work by herself at night. We nearly had a serious altercation after she said she wanted Margarite back on night duty. I couldn't let that happen so I..."

Lance folded his arms across his chest and looked at her, his gaze unwavering. "And you did what? Come on Janessa, out with it. Is this a jailable offense?"

She could feel heat creep into her face. "Of course not! I came home and called Leo Scutterby. I told him about Margarite and what Potts was trying to do. By the time I drove back to the hospital he had called her and Bully Bill. Margarite no longer has to work nights."

"At least you didn't hit her."

Janessa stifled a laugh. "No, but Potts is furious with me. She's wracking her brain to find a way to make Margarite work nights."

"Why does she want her working that shift?" Lance asked, clearly puzzled.

"That's a good question. I asked if she wanted Margarite alone and vulnerable so she could finish the job of killing her."

Chapter Eighteen

"That's it. You two need to stop sleuthing. This is not a game of hide and seek we're playing. We're trying to catch a murderer. It's dangerous and someone might get hurt. Leave the investigation to the professionals. How many times have I told you that?" Lance glanced back and forth between Janessa and Margarite. Neither woman said a word. "Do I make myself clear or do I have to lock you both up?"

Janessa looked horrified. "You can't do that. We haven't done anything wrong. What are the charges? Do we need a lawyer?"

A hint of a smile flickered across his face. "We could charge you with hindering a criminal investigation for one thing. I'm sure Pete and I could come up with a couple of others as well."

Janessa sighed and looked at Margarite. "Okay, we won't investigate. But what are we supposed to do if information falls into our laps?"

When Pete laughed, Lance followed suit. "That isn't likely to happen." Pete said as he struggled to contain his laughter. "If by chance information falls out of the air and into your vicinity, call us and we'll handle it. Okay?"

Still smirking, he and Lance said their goodbyes and left to go back on duty. Janessa went into the kitchen and put the kettle on for tea. "Those two have some nerve. They think information won't suddenly appear for us? I've got news for them. They don't know our sources. We still have to talk to Charlie and hear what he's found out."

Margarite left the sofa and joined Janessa in the kitchen. "But you just told the guys we wouldn't sleuth anymore. You lied to them."

"Not exactly," Janessa said as she put tea bags into two mugs. "My fingers were crossed behind my back, so that's not exactly lying, is it?"

Margarite laughed. "No, it isn't if you're six years old. Really, Janessa, what are we going to do if we can't investigate?"

"We're going to do the same things we've been doing. Ask questions and keep our eyes and ears open. Now, shall we call Charlie and see what tidbits of information he has for us? I don't consider that sleuthing. We're just going to have a conversation with your cousin." At that moment her phone rang. She almost put it on speaker, thinking it was Charlie calling.

"Janessa?"

"Hi Dad, what's up?"

"Your mother and I would like to invite you and Margarite to dinner on Saturday night if you're free. Mom is making her famous lasagna."

"Wow, I can taste it now. Margarite and I can make it, but I don't know if Lance and Pete will be free. I'll have to check with them."

"We're not asking them. We would like a dinner with just you two girls. Is that okay? We can ask your boyfriends another time. It's not that we don't want them here, it's just that we want to see you and Margarite, especially after her scare. Okay?"

"Sure, Dad," Janessa said, looking over at Margarite who was busy filling Brutus's water bowl. "What time would you like us to be there? Six?" She glanced at Margarite, who nodded. "Yes. We can be there at six. I hope there will be garlic bread too."

Her father laughed. "Mom says not to worry. She'll have all of your favorites, including garlic bread and a nice, crisp salad so you can get your veggies."

"Great. We'll see you on Saturday. I can smell the lasagna already. Talk to you later. Love you." She hung up the phone and eyed Margarite. "Something's up, inviting us for dinner isn't unusual, but no boyfriends? That's odd."

"Maybe not. What else did he say? You should have put it on speaker."

"I wasn't sure what he was going to say. You know how my dad can be sometimes. I thought I'd spare us both the embarrassment if he said something off color. He says they want to see us, especially after your ordeal."

"Maybe it's true. We'll find out when we get there, won't we? Lasagna? I can't wait. The anticipation will make the rest of the week go faster. I can even deal with Carla if I have something that good to look forward to, right?"

Janessa laughed. "Absolutely. Heaven knows what adventures she has in store for us for the rest of the week. Maybe nothing. That would be a pleasant change." Janessa's phone rang again. She looked at the screen and saw that this time it was Charlie calling. She put the phone on speaker, then answered. "Hey Charlie. The phone is on speaker. Margarite is here with me. Anything good come your way?"

"Oh yes." She could hear him chuckling. "I'll say it did. I still haven't pinpointed which one is Margarite's mother, but I know who isn't."

"Who?" Margarite shouted across the room. "Who? Charlie, come on, give."

"Whoa, hold on girl. In due time. My source said that she found out that Carla Potts is related, but she is not the baby mama. She is one of the aunties. It was her job to clean up the mess her sister got into and make sure the baby was adopted. She was also supposed to make sure no one knew where the kid was and that she was adopted far enough away so that no one would accidentally run into her in a supermarket or anything like that."

Janessa took a deep breath. "Charlie, what about April? Is she the mother?" She held her breath until he answered.

"Not according to my source, but that's not definite. The cousin says that she has more digging to do to find out if April gave birth, which is a definite possibility."

"What on earth was she doing at Ashton Community Hospital and who killed her?"

"I still don't have all the answers, but I am getting closer. As for the father, I don't have much on him. I guess the baby was a well-kept secret from everyone, including him. From what Margarite's cousin says, April never liked keeping the baby a secret from everyone and I think that included the father. I still don't know if he is aware that he has an adult daughter. Information about him is scarce."

Margarite leaned forward so she could get closer to the phone. "So, Potts is my aunt?"

"One of then, yes." Charlie said.

"Good grief, how many of them are there?" Janessa asked.

He chuckled. "I haven't determined that yet. There were several, including the cousin's mother, who is not the baby mama either. Listen girls, I'll stay on this until we find out what happened back then. We need to find out who gave birth to Margarite and who the father could be. The one thing you said that sticks in my mind is that April and Margarite looked enough alike to be sisters. Or mother and daughter."

Margarite gasped. "We don't know much more than we did when we started, do we?"

Janessa looked over at her. "Actually, we know quite a bit more." At Margarite's questioning gaze she said, "We know that Potts is not your mother, that April could be your mother and that you have a whole family out there that you haven't met yet. Where are these people living anyway? We've been talking about these faceless people for weeks, but I have no idea where they live. Are they in Massachusetts, Charlie?"

"Yes. Most of them live just outside of Boston, in the Somerville, Medford area. When Margarite was placed for adoption, they simply went to the neighboring state of Connecticut to adopt her out. It's fairly common for children to be placed in another state, but close to their birthplace. That's all I have for now. I'll call when I get more information. In the meantime, Margarite, stay safe. I don't want anything to happen to you now. You've been my cousin for a long time, and I've gotten attached to you."

"Thanks, Charlie," Margarite said, with tears leaking out of her eyes. "I love you, too."

"All right, kids, I'll talk to you both soon."

Janessa clicked the phone off and handed Margarite a tissue from a box on the nearby buffet, then got up to put a kettle on for more tea. She knew Margarite needed a few minutes to compose herself. April's death and her own close encounter had taken a toll on her. Finding out that she was related to Potts probably didn't help, but there wasn't anything she could do about that. She knew they had to decide how to approach Potts with this new information. She figured that Margarite would want to rush into the hospital and confront her, but they had to be careful. If Potts was the murderer, she'd find a way to get to Margarite, no matter how much she was protected. Janessa needed time to sort things out and decide on the best strategy.

She sat back down and looked at Margarite who sat, dry-eyed, staring into space. "Tell me what you're thinking. I know this is a lot to take in, and being related to Potts is probably a shock."

Margarite turned and focused on Janessa. "I want to scream in her face and ask her what she thinks she's doing. I want to ask her if she killed the woman who might be my mother and if she tried to strangle me to get me out of the way, as well."

"She won't get that chance again, if I can help it. She's not going to get that close to you. We have to keep a close eye on her, Griff and Franklin. Although I must say that Franklin has been scarce these days. I wonder where he's lurking about. I expect that he'll pop up any day now and begin making a nuisance of himself again."

"You're probably right. I'm still trying to wrap my head around the fact that I'm related to Potts, that she's my birth mother's sister. My aunt. What a legacy. I'm related to a lunatic and possibly a murderer. The joys of living my life."

"Hey, it could be worse."

Marguerite looked at her as if she was the one who'd lost her mind. "Really? How. How can it be any worse to be Potts's niece and to be in the cross hair of a murderer."

"Well, ah, look at the bright side. Potts isn't your mother although she could be the murderer or Franklin or Griff could be your father and either could be a murderer."

"What a bright light you've shone on the situation. Thanks. I thought you were my friend."

Janessa sighed. "I am your friend. I was trying to help, maybe make you see some humor in this whole crazy scenario. I wish something would break in this case, even if it means we don't solve it, but the police do the honors."

"As long as the something that breaks isn't me, I'll be happy. Now, I'd better go We have to work tomorrow and who knows what drama we'll have to deal with."

Janessa nodded and rose from her chair while Margarite did the same. "Let's go. I'll take you home." The work week was just beginning. Anything could happen. After dropping Margarite off at her apartment, Janessa drove back home. She went inside to an excited dog jumping up and down. After she replenished Brutus' water bowl she let him outside to take care of things. It was chilly outside so the little dog didn't fool around chasing things and sniffing at nothing. She considered going for a short walk, but decided she had to dig her heavier coat out of the closet first. She'd freeze in her light-weight jacket.

She rooted around in her closet until she found her warm, fleece jacket. She decided that she and Brutus could do with a short walk after all. After snapping Brutus' leash to his collar, the duo left Janessa's little house. She closed and locked the door, a new habit since her house had been ransacked and trashed by a crazed killer a year ago. She shook her head. It didn't seem like it was that long ago that Leo Scutterby's illegitimate daughter killed his other daughter. He'd become a good friend to Janessa after accusing her of his daughter's murder. She took a deep breath of the crisp fall air. Now they were dealing with it again. Only this time it wasn't her freedom that was at stake. It was Margarite's life. They'd been going around in circles for months with no clear answers. She and Margarite needed to catch the killer somehow.

Chapter Nineteen

The next day was bright, cold, and clear although a hint of snow persisted. There was minimal drama in the Critical Care Unit. The exception was a demented patient who insisted that her catheter was an intrusion into her personal space, and she continually pulled it out. Janessa finally convinced her to leave it alone after the fourth time when there was some undoubted tearing of the woman's sensitive area, followed by considerable pain and bleeding.

The rest of the week flew by, and before long Friday came and went. Saturday arrived and while Janessa didn't exactly dread having dinner with her parents, she had a feeling she wasn't going to like the lecture her father was sure to deliver about their sleuthing and the dangers involved. Heaven knew what he would say about her involving Leo Scutterby in their dispute with Carla Potts. There was a slim possibility that her father might be grateful that she hadn't dragged him into it, for once. Janessa resigned herself to the fact that there was no hope of wriggling out of the invitation. If she and Margarite didn't show up for dinner, she had no doubt that her father would track her down and the meeting would have severe consequences. It didn't matter that she was a 30-year-old grown woman. She was still his little girl, and she'd better listen to him.

After a quick cleaning of her house, she fed Brutus and took him for a short walk. He wouldn't be happy to be left alone tonight so she gave him an extra treat. Having finished all her household chores and settled her dog, she showered and prepared for the evening with her parents and Margarite. She opted for a casual look that could pass for day or evening, crisp dark gray slacks paired with a light pearl, gray silk blouse. A pair of Jimmy Choo gunmetal/silver stilettos completed her outfit. She normally wouldn't wear this type of shoe, but after being in nursing clogs all week, she felt these would give her confidence to face her father's undoubted wrath. She let her mass of curls frame her face instead of being confined in her usual topknot. After adding a pair of sterling silver hoop earrings to her ensemble, and she was ready to face the evening. When a knock sounded on the door accompanied by the doorbell ring, she knew it was Margarite. They'd decided to ride together in Margarite's car. Janessa opened the door and couldn't hold back the peal of laughter. Except for the fact that Margarite's outfit was a pair of black slacks paired with an emerald, green silk blouse, which brought out the green in her eyes, it looked like they'd purposely coordinated their outfits right down to the Jimmy Choos on Margarite's feet. Hers were black, as were the hoops in her ears. Her auburn hair hung in loose waves.

"We look marvelous, don't we?" Janessa said with a grin. She stepped back so that Margarite could come into the room. Margarite wore a black pea coat, which matched the grey one Janessa had decided to wear. She saw Margarite eyeing it then looked down at her own. Janessa laughed. "Yes, it is an Ann Klein. I got it on sale at Macy's last year."

"Wow," Margarite said. "We shop alike. I got mine there too and yes mine is also Ann Klein. I figured that I'd better wear a warmer coat since I saw some snowflakes earlier."

"Bite your tongue. It's much too early for snow. I'm glad my parent's house isn't that far from here. Unlike your parents, we don't have to travel across the state to visit."

"Hey," Margarite said, laughing. "My parents aren't that far away. It's only a couple of hours to their house. They're only in Connecticut, not Alaska."

"True, but on a night like this I'd rather not drive that far. My parents are just outside of Ashton, in Bruxton. Ready?"

The women walked to Margarite's car. It was bigger than Janessa's Mini Cooper, so they'd decided to take the bigger car. They slid into the seats, which had cooled off while Margarite was in Janessa's house. "Whoa, turn up the heat on these seats before my everything freezes."

"We need to give the car a minute or two to heat up." After waiting a few seconds, Margarite reached over and hit a couple of buttons. Warmth flooded through Janessa.

"That's more like it."

A short time later they arrived at the two-story brick Colonial Janessa's parents had bought in the 90s. They had completely renovated it, so the interior could pass for a layout in *Better Homes and Gardens* magazine. They parked in front of the garage and walked the short distance to the front door. After ringing the doorbell, Janessa waved, knowing they were on the doorbell's camera. She heard her father laugh as he opened the door then enveloped her in a warm hug. Jerome Williams was a big man. He stood about 6 feet 6 and weighed over two hundred pounds, however there was no fat on his body. He was big, but lean and in shape from his daily workouts. His bald head shone in the light, making him look intimidating, but Janessa knew he doted on her and her mother. Janessa's mother was short in comparison at 5 feet 6 inches. She was trim, with medium length hair styled in braids, making her look younger than her 65 years.

They strolled into the entryway onto the polished wood floors. The staircase led to the second story where there was a master suite and a smaller room that had been Janessa's growing up. After she'd grown up, she had asked her parents if they would be downsizing. The prompt answer was no. The finished basement was 20 ft x 20 ft, and, other than the furnace and some pipes, her mother claimed the rest of the basement as her craft/sewing room. In her youth, Janessa's mother had been a seamstress for some of the big couture houses in New York City. Content to stay home and raise her daughter, she'd given that up when

Janessa was born. She still, however, sewed her own designer wardrobe as well as the occasional piece for Janessa.

Her father hugged Margarite then it was her mother's turn. After hugging both women he led the way into the living area, which opened to a glassed-in porch. It was getting too cold to sit out there so the French doors leading to that area were closed.

Janessa and Margarite each took a seat in the two off-white occasional chairs, strategically placed for visitors to enjoy the view. Janessa's parents sat on the matching sofa facing them. "Dinner is almost ready. Would either of you like a drink?"

"Just water for me, Mom. It's been a long week and any alcohol would likely put me to sleep."

Janessa said.

Margarite agreed and opted for water as well, especially since she was the driver. "I'm happy you and Dr. Williams decided not to downsize and sell this beautiful home," she said, looking at the older couple.

"We are too," said Janessa's mother. She turned toward her husband and nodded. "I'm going to finish getting the food ready," she said as she turned to go into the kitchen.

"Is there anything I can do to help, Mom?" Janessa asked.

"No, honey. Just relax and talk to your father."

Janessa's father cleared his throat and leaned forward. "Janessa, honey, I know you mean well and that you want to protect Margarite, but this sleuthing has to stop. One or both of you will get hurt. Look what has happened to Margarite already. The police are on this case. Let Pete and Lance do their jobs. You don't need to investigate. They are more than capable of catching whoever is trying to hurt Margarite."

Janessa stared at her father. Deep down she knew that what he was saying made sense, but she also had enough of her father in her to want to rebel. "The guys can handle this, and I know that, but I can help. I know the people at the hospital, who is supposed to be where, doing whatever and sometimes the places and the players don't add up. I figured this little talk was why you didn't invite the guys to join us for dinner. We already got the lecture from Lance and Pete. Have you been collaborating with them? They want me to stay out if the investigation too. Can't you see that I need to do this?"

"Janessa Sherie Williams! You don't have to do anything except be the wonderful nurse that you are. Let the police handle this. I don't want anything to happen to you or Margarite. And no, I haven't spoken to Lance or Pete, but we all want what's best for you."

She knew she was in trouble when he used her complete name. She felt about ten years old when he did that. "But Dad!"

"No buts young lady. You heard what I said. And I won't even get into why you felt you had to involve Leo Scutterby in your investigation."

"Oh. That's easy to explain. Carla Potts was intent on making Margarite work the day after someone tried to kill her. Not day, night. The night after she was almost killed. She wasn't even out of the Critical Care Unit when that woman started harping on Margarite's return to work. That made me suspicious. Why was she so insistent that Margarite work the next night. She would have been alone again. That was a dangerous situation. I didn't want to get you involved in the fiasco, so I called the only other person I thought could help me, Leo."

"She wanted her to return to work that soon? I wasn't given that piece of information. I'm not condoning what you did by calling Leo, but I think it was the right thing to do. However, don't ever think you can't come to me in a crisis."

"I know Dad, you've always been there. I should have known Carla would run to you with her grievances. She's a real piece of work and I..."

"Dinner is ready," her mother called from the dining room. "No more discussion unless it's pleasant. Understand?"

Margarite nodded and smiled at Janessa's mother. "Okay, Mom. Discussion over," Janessa said.

The meal was exactly the way Janessa wanted it. The lasagna was flavorful, and the garlic bread melted in her mouth. "You've out done yourself, Mom. I'm too full to move right now."

Her mother smiled. "No room for cheesecake?"

"You're killing me Mrs. Williams," Margarite said with a groan. "Double time on the treadmill tomorrow. That makes all of this," She gestured to the table, "worthwhile."

"I agree. I'm glad you asked us over. The food was so delicious I didn't even mind the lecture." Janessa said.

Everyone laughed, then Janessa and Margarite stood and cleared the table. After loading the dishwasher, they settled back down at the table for dessert. "Mom, this cheesecake is fantastic. You make the creamiest in the world. It's even better than the ones you can get in New York City. I'm in heaven," Janessa said as she savored another bite.

"You say that every time, but honey, I don't mind your repetition at all. I'll take all the compliments I can get."

After a few chuckles and further compliments, the girls cleared the dessert dishes. After they drank coffee, it was time for Margarite and Janessa to leave. The women said a brief goodnight to Janessa's, then walked to Margarite's car, shivering in the colder night air.

They slid into their seats and Margarite started the car. "I guess the lecture wasn't too bad. My father has a valid point. I don't want us to get hurt either."

Margarite nodded. "True. Does that mean we're done sleuthing?"

"No way. We just got some new information. Why would we stop now? Bite your tongue, girl. We've only just begun. So, I was thinking that when we go back to work on Monday, depending on how many patients we have, I can do some sleuthing."

"Okay," Margarite said, slowing down to turn into Janessa's driveway. "Do you have a plan in mind or are we just going to wing it?"

Janessa grinned although she knew Margarite couldn't see her in the dark interior of the car. "Of course I have a plan. Don't I always?"

"I was afraid you'd say that. Okay, what is your plan, and do I have to do anything I'm not going to like? Never mind, forget I asked that. You always make me do something I don't like."

Janessa gave a loud sigh. "Ah Margarite, this time you're wrong. All you have to do is stay in the Critical Care Unit and take care of any patients we have. Hopefully it will only be one or two because I'm going to have to leave you alone on the floor for a short time."

"What? You're leaving me alone?" Margarite's voice was a squeak.

"Not for long. It's just for a little while. It won't take me long to do what I have to do."

"And what is that? Is it something that can wait until after work?"

"Not really. I want to scope out downstairs and investigate Potts' office for any clues."

"You what?" Margarite yelled. No more squeak. "You can't do that! If you get caught, she can fire you on the spot and then what will happen to me. I'll tell you what. Without your protection someone will come along and kill me, that's what will happen to me."

Janessa reached over and patted her friend's arm. "Nothing will happen to you. There will be other people bustling around. No one will dare try anything while I'm gone."

"You don't know that. I'm worried about this plan of yours. I'm scared too." She stopped the car and turned off the engine. Janessa opened the passenger door and prepared to get out. "There are so many things that could go wrong."

Janessa got out of the car and leaned on the door. "Nothing will go wrong. We'll be fine. It won't take me long. I have the code for the supervisor's office so I can get in with no trouble."

"How did you get that? You're not a supervisor or the Chief Nursing Officer."

"It's better if you don't know how I got the code, Margarite. Trust me when I say that we have a lot of friends at the hospital and they're loyal to us, not Potts."

"I hope you know what you're doing so we both don't get killed or at the very least, fired."

"I'll call you tomorrow and finalize our plans," Janessa said as she closed the car door. She looked back and waved as Margarite backed out of the driveway and drove away.

Chapter Twenty

Sunday morning dawned clear and cold. Janessa made a half a pot of coffee then called Margarite. "Want to go to church with me this morning?"

"Sure. I love Reverend James' sermons. He gets directly to the point but not in a holier than thou, pardon the pun, preachy way. I've already showered. Let me put some clothes on, I'll be there in ten minutes. That gives us half an hour before church starts."

"Great. I made a half a pot of coffee so come in and help yourself. I haven't showered yet, but it won't take me long."

Before long, Janessa was showered and dressed and walked into the kitchen just as Margarite finished her coffee. *Giving her a key is the best thing I've ever done.* She congratulated herself on her foresight as she poured the rest of the coffee in her mug and downed the tepid brew. "Ready?" She grinned at Margarite. "After church we can come back here for brunch if you want, and we can discuss tomorrow."

"I'm always up for a good brunch. What are we having?"

Janessa laughed. "Good question. I have some eggs and potatoes, and I believe I also have some bacon and or sausage."

"Good. We'll splurge and have both. I killed my treadmill last night when I got home from your parent's house."

"That's so funny. I did the same thing. I put Brutus out before you got here. Let me get him inside, then we can head to church." Janessa said as she opened the back door for her dog. He danced around Margarite's legs as if he was hoping she'd pick him up, but he'd been in the yard in dirt and whatever, so she patted his head. He flopped down with a sigh, ignoring his water and food bowls. "I guess he's completely outraged that you won't pick him up and cuddle. Poor Brutus," Janessa crouched down and rubbed his ears. "We'll be back in a little while. After church Auntie Mags will pick you up. Dirty paws won't matter then." She straightened and headed for the door. "Be back soon, Brutus." She called as she closed the door behind her and Margarite.

Reverend James' sermon was inspiring as always and the women agreed they were glad they'd attended. The fact that Janessa's parents hovered nearby wasn't a deterrent at all. She and Margarite were frequent attendees so her parents couldn't berate her for being faithless. They waited outside the church doors for her parents to emerge. Both women hugged Janessa's parents, then moved out of the way of other parishioners who were leaving the church.

"What are you two girls planning to do today?" Janessa's father asked, smiling down at them.

"Just a quick brunch and a cuddle with Brutus. The guys are on duty today, but they might drop by later. They said they'd try. How about you? Any plans? A leisurely afternoon with the TV, Dad? Sewing a new outfit, Mom?"

"We wish," they said simultaneously, then laughed. Janessa's father put his arm around her mother and pulled her close. "No, the Birches are coming for lunch. They'll spend the afternoon, so it's a little different from our usual routine."

"We don't mind though." Her mother was quick to add. "We don't have a lot of company these days, so it will be nice."

Janessa hugged her parents then she and Margarite climbed into Margarite's car and left the church parking lot. "We'd better hope my parents are too busy to check and see if we're sleuthing today."

"Is that what we're doing? I thought we were having a nice quiet brunch and watching TV or something until the men show up."

Janessa laughed. "That's kind of what we're doing. Brunch and we'll turn the TV on so that if the guys come there unexpectedly, they might not hear what we're talking about."

Margarite smiled, but instead of turning to look at Janessa, she stared straight ahead at the road. A few errant snowflakes started drifting down. "We're not supposed to get anything significant, are we?"

Janessa peered out of the passenger window. "Not as far as I know. It seems kind of early for a big snowstorm. We haven't had Thanksgiving yet, but this is the Berkshires, so you never know. Anything could happen. If it starts coming down heavier, we'll have to postpone brunch."

She saw Margarite grimace. "I hope not. I'm starving. What's on the menu again?"

"Eggs Benedict and avocado toast and tea or coffee. Your choice."

"Wow, when did you decide that? I thought we were just having eggs and sausage or bacon. You know how to treat a girl right. My two favorites."

As they got close to Janessa's house, they spotted Lance and Pete sitting in Lance's car in the driveway. Margarite parked beside them. "So much for discussing our plans for tomorrow." Janessa muttered under her breath. Not that she wasn't happy to see Lance, but the days went smoothly if she and Margarite had a chance to plan what they were going to do. They would have to call each other later.

"I hope you have plenty of eggs," Margarite said, after putting the car in Park.

The women got out of the car as did the men. "This is a pleasant surprise. We weren't expecting you until later." Janessa said.

Lance hugged Janessa and gave her a brief kiss. Pete did the same to Margarite and the two couples moved toward Janessa's front door where they could hear Brutus yapping. "I'm sure he knows all of his favorite people are here," Janessa said as she fit her key into the door lock.

"Either that or he has to go to the bathroom really bad." Lance laughed.

"Or both," Pete chimed in.

As soon as Janessa got the door opened, the little tornado jumped up into her arms and covered her face with doggy kisses. He spotted Margarite and did the same to her. Lance and Pete were next, and when he was done handing out doggy love, Lance put him outside into the fenced backyard so he could take care of his business.

Janessa filled Brutus' water bowl while Margarite made coffee. The women joined forces to get the breakfast on the table and by an unspoken agreement the men cleared the table and loaded the dishwasher when they were finished eating. Sitting around the living room with cups of coffee or tea, everyone had a full belly and was content with the silence until Lance spoke.

"Remember what I said ladies. No more sleuthing. Stay low key tomorrow and call us immediately if anything doesn't look or feel right. You're up against a ruthless killer and we still aren't sure who it is. The evidence leads us one way, then something happens that contradicts everything we've learned."

Janessa snuggled close to him in the oversized chair they were sharing. "We know it could be dangerous. Whoever the killer is, they've already attacked Margarite once. We certainly don't want to take a chance on that happening again." She smiled at Margarite who was cuddled close to Pete on the sofa. "What do you guys have planned for the rest of the day?" she asked, turning to look at Lance. Both men turned a bright shade of red. After a moment of silence, Lance stuttered. "We umm, have to do some things."

Pete said "paperwork" at the same time. With a sheepish look at Pete, Lance cleared his throat and said, "That's right. We have some paperwork and things like that to do. Actually, I think we'd better head back to the station." He stood, and Pete followed suit. After they left, Janessa glanced at Margarite and said, "What do you think that was all about? I don't believe for a minute that they have paperwork to do. They know something and they don't want us to know what. But that's okay, sooner or later one of them will spill the beans. In the meantime, let's talk about our strategy for tomorrow."

Margarite pulled back the curtain by the front door. "I think not. It's snowing pretty heavy outside. I should go now before the roads get bad. I'll call you when I get home."

Janessa looked out the window as well. "Wow, Margarite. I didn't realize it was snowing so hard." She helped Margarite with her coat and ushered her out the door. "Be careful and call me the minute you get home."

Margarite waved then slid into her car. Luckily, she lived close and although the snow was falling hard, the roads still looked clear. Janessa closed the door as a blast of cold wind whipped through the room. Lance had let Brutus in from the backyard, so she checked his water bowl then settled in front of the TV with a cup of tea. Her mind was not on the show. Instead, she was going through a list of scenarios that could happen when she and Margarite went to work the next day. The day seemed to speed by. After cleaning up the few dishes that were in the sink and sweeping the floor, Janessa decided to take a shower and go to bed early. She hadn't come to any conclusions about what would happen the next day.

As she headed down the hall, her cell phone rang. "I'm home. It wasn't bad until just before I got here. It's starting to stick on the road now. Why don't I pick you up tomorrow? We'll never get there in the mini if there's a significant amount of snow."

"Hey, I'll have you know my little car can go through the biggest piles of snow."

Margarite laughed. "Have you ever tried it?"

"Well not exactly, but I know it can. I haven't come up with any bright ideas about tomorrow, so I guess we'll play it by ear when we get there." Conceding defeat she said, "Okay, pick me up, tomorrow. I don't want to clog up my tires with snow."

Margarite was still laughing when they said goodbye. She checked a second time that her door was locked, let Brutus out for the last time that night and laughed while he barked at the snow and tried to catch it on his tongue. Janessa continued down the hall to take a nice hot shower after she let him back in and topped off his water.

Chapter Twenty-one

"Remember, Margarite. If anyone is looking for me, tell them I have a stomach problem and I'm in the bathroom. Mrs. Claremont should be moved soon, but I won't be gone very long. You should be safe."

The Critical Care Unit's only patient was being moved to the medical unit. Janessa was sure that if anyone tried to hurt Margarite she would scream loud and long. With a small backward wave, Janessa walked through the double doors and pushed the button for the elevator. When she arrived on the first floor where the offices were, she looked around to make sure no one was nearby. She glanced at her fitness watch. It was nearly noon so most of the office personnel should be heading to lunch, including Carla Potts. Looking around a second time, she walked to the door of the supervisor's office. She tried not to hurry. She didn't want to attract attention.

When Janessa tapped in the code, the door opened. She rifled through the drawers, lifted items off the shelf to look behind them and scanned any area she thought Carla might hide information. She figured that Carla must have her purse with her because it was not in the room. After she decided that Carla hadn't left any information in the office, she figured she'd better leave before someone came. Just then she heard the click of the code being put in the door. With seconds to spare she squeezed into a small cupboard near the desk. *Thank my DNA that I'm small.* She barely fit. Her knees were jammed into her chest making it difficult to breathe. *This was a really bad idea. Margarite said it was, and I should have paid attention to her warning for once.* Janessa listened intently to see who had come into the office.

It was Becca Doane, the CNO. When she began talking on the phone, Janessa thought she would suffocate if this turned out to be a long conversation. Luckily for her the call was short. As soon as she heard the door open and slam shut, she crawled out of the cabinet and stood. Her legs trembled and refused to move, but she had to get out of the office before anyone else came in. She cracked the door open and peeked out. After racing to the elevator, she slammed her hand against the button to go up to the Critical Care Unit. She'd been gone a lot longer than she intended.

She got off the elevator and nearly ran into the Unit. She stopped short when she saw that there was no one at the nurse's station. *Hmmm. Margarite is either over on the medical/surgical unit or maybe the bathroom.* Janessa checked the room the patient, Mrs. Claremont had occupied. She was gone and so was Margarite. She hurried to the end of the hall and checked the restroom. The door was open, so obviously Margarite wasn't there. She glanced into the cardiac rehab room, but it was empty. Telling herself not to panic did no good. She'd already passed that stage. Taking a deep breath, she went to the medical/ surgical unit to see if Margarite was there.

"Hi Janine," she said, addressing the nurse at the front desk of the medical/surgical unit. "Is Margarite still here? I know she was supposed to transfer Mrs. Claremont to you."

Janine frowned when she looked up at Janessa. "No, she gave us a report on the patient then she left. I assumed she was going back to the Critical Care Unit. Isn't she there?"

Janessa could feel a flush creeping into her face. *Where is Margarite? I never should have left her alone.* She fled to the stairs without answering Janine. She ran back into the Critical Care Unit to check one more time to see if Margarite had returned. The Unit was empty. She pulled her phone out of her pocket and called the police. Her hands were shaking. She was panting and could barely speak. "Detective Halen or Detective Cranston, please." Lance answered.

"Hi honey, what's up?"

"He's got her, Lance. He's got her and he's going to kill her."

"Slow down and tell me what's happening. Who's got whom?"

"M-margarite. She's gone. I was stupid. I left her alone in the Unit and now I can't find her. I know he's got her, and he's going to kill her."

"We'll be right there. Stay where you are until we get there."

"No, I know it's Griff Lewis and I know where he's taken her. No one would know where she was or hear her scream in there."

"Where, Janessa? Where would he take her?"

"The boiler room. It's in the back of the hospital so it's secluded. No one would know, except me. I made safety rounds with him the other day and we had to inspect the boiler room. He's got her. Please hurry!"

"Wait, Janessa stay where you are. Let us..."

She hung up and fled to the stairs. She couldn't wait for Lance and Pete to get there. It might already be too late for Margarite. She hesitated on the stairs, and not watching where she was going, she ran into a male chest. She looked up, terrified, then angry. "Griff, where is she? What have you done to Margarite?" Tears were streaming down her cheeks. She swiped at them with a fist, but more gushed out. She punched Griff in the chest and screamed at him. "Bring her back! Where is she? You'd better not have hurt her."

Griff grabbed her wrists and held her so she would stop hitting him. "Stop. I haven't seen Margarite. Stand still and talk to me."

Janessa stopped and stared at him. "You, what do you mean you haven't seen her? You must have. I can't find her anywhere. You must have taken her."

"No," Griff said. "I've been at the dentist's office for over two hours this morning." He patted his cheek. "See? Gauze, for the blood."

At that moment she realized that he was telling the truth. The words coming from his mouth sounded thick and slurred. He said "dentist" as if it was spelled with a 'th' at the end. Nothing made sense. Who had Margarite if it wasn't Griff?

"Then who? Oh my God. It has to be Carla Potts or Franklin Stevens. I think I know exactly where she's taken her. Follow me. Remember what you said the other day about the boiler room? You said that no one goes in there unless you send them. Carla would know that."

"It's not Franklin. I can vouch for him. He's no killer," Griff said.

Janessa and Griff ran the rest of the way down the stairs. They stopped at the door leading into the boiler room. Griff's lecture the day they'd done safety rounds played over and over in her mind. *"No one but me comes in here to check unless I send them. You could sit in the chair at that desk and sleep, play music or do whatever you want. No one can hear through these walls."* She motioned that she was going to ease the door open and that he should stay silent. She was terrified of what she'd find on the other side of the heavy door. As quietly as she could, she pulled it toward her. She spotted Carla Potts who was so focused on Margarite that she apparently didn't hear them coming into the room.

Margarite sat in the chair, facing the door, her eyes wide with fright. Janessa held a finger up to caution her not to let on that she and Griff were in the room. A scarf was tied in a slip knot around Margarite's neck. Carla stood off to the side of her and had one end of the scarf. She was twirling it in her hand. With every twirl the scarf tightened. Janessa could see Margarite beginning to struggle for air.

"Carla, let her go!" Janessa yelled startling the older woman. Instead of dropping the scarf, she tightened it more. "You can't kill all three of us. Let her go. The police are on their way."

"By the time the police get here, she'll be dead. I really don't care if I go to jail. Between her and that little tramp April, they ruined everything. I planned it. I got rid of the baby and covered all traces of it so no one would know where she'd been taken." She looked at Margarite. "When you started working here, I wanted to kill you, but at first you seemed to mind your own business. Then she," Carla nodded toward Janessa, "decided to snoop around April's murder so I knew I had to act. I almost had you, but that bumbling idiot Griff had to choose that moment to show up. I barely got out of there without him seeing me."

Janessa signaled behind her back for Griff to slowly move to her right side while she moved up closer to Carla at a 45-degree angle to the left. *I need to move fast enough to block her from pulling the scarf tighter around Margarite's neck.* She crept closer. She saw that Carla was ranting and losing control, so she was more dangerous than ever. Janessa took a deep breath and focused. Her gaze met Margarite's terrified one. She tilted her head down, signaling for Margarite to do the same. That would make it harder for Carla to tighten the scarf.

As a struggle ensued, Janessa kicked the side of Carla's knee as hard as she could. As soon as Carla broke her hold on the scarf, Margarite raised herself up and slammed the heel of her hand into the woman's chin. There was an audible *crack* as Carla's teeth smashed together. Free of the scarf Margarite stood and ran toward the door. Griff ran around to Carla's other side and grabbed her arms, wrenching them behind her back. Janessa was about to call 911 when she remembered there was no signal in the boiler room. Running to the door, she slammed it open in time to see the police headed by detectives Halen and Cranston running down the stairs.

Janessa held the door for them and heard Carla being read her Miranda rights as she was led away in handcuffs. Griff was reaching for the scarf that had been wrapped around Margarite's neck when Detective Halen yelled, "Stop. That's evidence. Don't touch it."

"But it's my scarf," he said.

"We'll give it back when we've finished processing it."

Janessa exchanged a look with Griff. She grabbed Margarite and gave her a fierce hug. "Carla used your scarf, Griff, to try and frame you for Margarite's murder. Do you really want it back?"

"No, I guess not. I have something to show you Detective Halen. I'm going to reach into my pocket." He pulled out a card and handed it to the detective. Lance glanced at it then handed it to Janessa. She and Margarite stared at it then at Griff. GL, Private Investigative Services, the card read. She handed the card back to Griff. "Why didn't you tell us?"

"I couldn't," he said. "I was hired by the family to protect Margarite right after they learned of April's death. They knew Carla would be after her too. If April hadn't shown up here, she might not have decided to eliminate Margarite, but April triggered her by coming here and threatening to tell everything. Carla couldn't allow that because of all the underhanded things she had done to conceal Andrea's baby."

"Andrea, my mother's name is Andrea?" Margarite asked, in a shocked whisper.

"Yes, Andrea Tomes. Unfortunately, she has no idea what happened to your father. He didn't know about you. Carla might have gotten rid of him, too, but your mother can tell you more than I can."

Janessa stared; her mouth gaped open until Margarite gently tapped a finger under her chin to close it. "You mean my mother is alive?"

"Yes, no thanks to your aunt. She tried to get rid of her also, but your mother's been guarded round the clock until we could apprehend Carla. I had to wait for her to make her move before I could say or do anything. Good thing Janessa was here keeping an eye on you. She saved your life. I'm sorry I wasn't here sooner. We've suspected Carla for a while."

"I think we saved her together." Janessa said. At that moment Franklin Stevens burst into the room. "Where is she? Is Margarite okay?"

Griff put up a hand to stop him from running over to the women. "She's fine, no thanks to you. Some back up you are. If it wasn't for Janessa, Margarite might not be here. I told you I had a dental appointment. Where were you when you should have been keeping an eye on the situation like I asked you to?"

Franklin shuffled his feet and looked down. "Sorry, boss, first Carla sent me to take care of a mindless task in the shed out back. Then, I was talking to one of the other housekeepers about an issue with one of the bathrooms on the first floor. It seems like someone deliberately threw a towel in there to cause a backup."

Griff made a sound of disgust. "A bathroom whisperer. It was probably Carla."

A nervous laugh filtered through the room. "Boss? Is he?" asked Lance.

"I hate to admit it, but yes, Franklin works for me and was *supposed* to be my back up." He looked over at Janessa. "I don't suppose I can entice you away from the hospital and offer you a job can I?"

Lance, who had crossed the room and had an arm around each of the women gave a short laugh. "No way. She's staying right here. She's a great nurse and I can keep her out of trouble if she's working here. Now, if I can just convince her that sleuthing is a job that should be left to the police." He looked at Griff. "and the Private Investigators, of course."

Chapter Twenty-Two

L ater that evening, Margarite, Griff, Franklin and detectives Halen and Cranston met at Janessa's house. They settled in with coffee, prepared to hear what Griff had to say relating to Carla Potts and why she tried to murder Margarite.

"Why, Griff? Why was Carla so intent on killing me?" Margarite asked.

"Margarite, your family has a good deal of money. That's why we had people protecting your mother. For Carla, it was never about the money. It was about the family name and avoiding scandal at all costs. Carla is the oldest of six girls. April was the youngest and your mother falls somewhere in the middle. When she got pregnant with you, the family was upset and uncertain what to do. She was 16 years old. The man, as far as I could gather was about 25 and back then it just wasn't the thing in that family to marry someone older with no resources and have a baby. He disappeared before he could be jailed for statutory rape. Your mother said it was consensual, but she was still a child. So, Andrea was kept in seclusion by Carla until you were born. As soon as you were able to leave the hospital, she took you away and no one knew where you were," he said looking at Margarite. "I was hired when it became apparent that Carla was coming unhinged. She tried to kill Andrea, luckily without success. She denied it. But there was a witness..."

"April." Janessa said.

"Yes, April. We tracked you, Margarite, to Ashton Community Hospital several years ago. It was okay until April heard Andrea crying that she wanted to see her baby one-time before she died."

Margarite's hand flew to her mouth. When tears trickled down her face, Janessa patted her arm and held her hand. Pete Cranston flanked her other side with his arm around her shoulders. He pulled her close.

"Andrea was ill at the time, but she's okay now." Griff assured her.

"Why didn't you let the police know about this? We might have been able to mitigate the circumstances and protect Margarite better," Lance asked.

"I wanted to, but at that point we couldn't prove that Carla killed April or even that she was the one who attacked Margarite. Unfortunately, we had to wait. Thankfully, Janessa was suspicious of Carla all along. If she hadn't been there to stop Carla, we wouldn't be sitting here now."

"Was there a reason you decided to do the safety tour in the boiler room?" Janessa asked.

"Yes, there was." Griff answered.

"We wanted you to be aware of the most unlikely and underutilized room in the hospital. Griff figured that if our hunch was correct and Carla grabbed Margarite, she'd take her someplace few people would know about and where no one would be able to hear her," Franklin said.

'Your hunch was right. Before you showed up, I remembered you saying that no one ever accessed that room unless you sent them there. At that time, I thought you were the murderer, so I felt you would take Margarite there. That's when I called the police and ran into you on the stairs. I was so worried about her. I was angry enough to push you down the stairs, but I needed to know where she was and if she was okay."

"Thank goodness you didn't. Carla had my scarf around Margarite's neck. She wanted to frame me for her murder, without knowing who I was." Griff said, grimacing.

"I'm still confused about why Carla killed April," Margarite said looking at Griff.

"April found out where you were. She didn't need proof that you were Andrea's daughter. You bear a resemblance to her, but you and

April looked more alike. She knew what Carla was capable of. She was trying to get to you to tell you everything and warn you about Carla. I guess she wasn't strong enough to fight her off," Griff speculated.

"She was my aunt, and she died trying to save me." Tears streamed down Margarite's face. "I wish I could have gotten to know her." Janessa handed her a tissue and she wiped her face. "And my mother? Does she know all of this?"

Griff looked uncomfortable, but he smiled, then answered. "Yes, she does. She told me Franklin and I had better keep you safe or we'd feel her wrath. After your first attack she was adamant that we stay even closer to you. We fell down on the job, but Janessa never wavered. She's as determined as your birth mother."

"Speaking of mothers, Margarite," Janessa said. "Have you called yours? She must be beside herself with worry."

"I called her as soon as it was all over. She and my dad are on their way here from Connecticut. My brother would have come with them, but he had another commitment. He'll be here tomorrow." She smiled. "My mom said she would help me get in touch with Andrea. She said it's about time we all met."

"I'm happy Becca was able to find someone to take over the Critical Care Unit for us. Maybe we've underestimated her and she's not as uncaring and self-absorbed as we thought."

Margarite laughed. "Nah, she doesn't want us suing Ashton Community Hospital so she's covering her butt. After all she's the one who was directly responsible for Carla's actions."

A few hours later they ordered pizza and sat around talking. When the doorbell rang Janessa peeked around the curtain to see who was there. Her eyes opened wide, and she turned to Margarite. "I think your mother is here."

"I know, I told you she and dad were on their way."

"No, Margarite. Not that mother. I think it's your birth mother. You look like her and there are men flanking her on either side." She looked at Griff. "Exactly how rich is this woman?"

Griff shrugged and smiled, so Janessa turned and opened the door. "Hi, I'm Janessa Williams." She thrust her hand toward the older woman. "You must be Andrea. I'm so happy to meet you. Come right in. We've been waiting for you."

THE END

Other books by Nanci Race:

Code Blue Murder

About the Author

Nanci Race was born in a small city in Western, Massachusetts, the second of six children born to a middleclass family of Native American descent. Her family moved when she was young, to the area known as The Berkshires, also in Western, Massachusetts. She began writing at a young age and even won contests for her poetry when she was in middle school. Although she was encouraged to write by her English teacher, she pursued a career in nursing. Fast forward many years when taking a hiatus from nursing Nanci became the editor of a magazine on the arts. That led to a BA degree in Creative Writing and Literature which she started at Southern Vermont College.

After being dually enrolled in Berkshire Community College and Charter Oak State College, two and a half years after starting her journey, she graduated from Charter Oak State in Connecticut.

Nanci returned to nursing for several years, but she was also working on her writing. Eventually many years after completing her BA, she returned to school and within two years had completed her Master of Fine Arts Degree with a concentration in Writing at Lindenwood University in St. Charles Missouri. These days, Nanci is retired from over forty years of nursing and loves spending time with her family, particularly attending her grandchildren's sporting events with her husband. She also is an avid sewist, having spent several years as co-owner of a sewing/tailoring store. In addition to sewing and reading, she enjoys almost all needle arts and travels whenever possible. Nanci currently has stories on the Kindle Vella platform.

Nanci is currently the President of Outreach International

Writers, inc. and is a member of Romance Writers of America having served as president of RWA's mystery and suspense chapter, KOD. She is a member of member of Contemporary Romance Writers and a past President of Capital Region RWA.

You can contact Nanci here: nphill5337817@gmail.com

www.ingramcontent.com/pod-product-compliance
Lightning Source LLC
Chambersburg PA
CBHW050938120626
46552CB00001B/264